THE DUKE'S MOONLIT SEDUCTION

A STEAMY REGENCY ROMANCE

EMME ALBRIGHT

KKI
PUBLISHING

THE DUKE'S MOONLIT SEDUCTION: A STEAMY REGENCY ROMANCE

Published by KKI Publishing, LLC
New Canaan, CT

Paperback ISBN: 979-8-9884468-0-4
Hardcover ISBN: 979-8-9884468-1-1

FICTION / Romance / Historical / Regency

This is a work of fiction. All of the characters, organizations, and events portrayed in this novel are either products of the author's imagination or are used fictitiously.

PROLOGUE

$\mathcal{T}$he little girl had escaped her mamma's loving clutches and made her way to the stables unnoticed by all, running as fast as her legs would carry her across the great lawn. As she got closer, she slowed her pace and crept as quietly as she could, avoiding windows and doors so the foreman and groomsman would not spot her and send her back to the main house. Fortunately for her, Tad, the Martin's trusted groomsman was nowhere in sight, so the girl snuck down the line of stables to her favorite horse. She cooed softly, whispering to him as he bent his head over the gate.

"Hello, Sebastian. Are you ready for me boy?" She removed her dress and carelessly threw it to the corner of the stall atop a hay bale. Dressed only in chemise and petticoats, the girl pushed her blonde plait aside, dispensing with the white bow her mother so carefully weaved into her long locks this morning. Being quite short, the girl thought to drag over another hay bale to make mounting the horse easier. Finally sitting confidently on the large beast, the girl clicked her tongue softly and set Sebastian forward with a little twitch of her heels at his side. They set forth with not a backward glance, Sebastian's hooves flying across the great lawn toward the pond nestled deep within her family's acreage.

The boy had been sitting for the last hour, methodically throwing stones into the water and watching, enraptured, at the ensuing ripples. He had made his escape from his newly appointed guardian's home as soon as decorum allowed so he could be alone to cry, frustrated and bereft over the loss of his beloved father. They had buried him only a few days earlier at their home, here at Ramsgate where the boy and his father lived together in a grand mansion overlooking the beautiful sea, and far from the bustling crowds and noise of London. Because the boy's mother had passed away during childbirth, his father had made arrangements years ago that should the boy be orphaned before his seventeenth birthday he be sent to stay with their closest friends, the Martins who also summered at Ramsgate, until such time as he could assume the duties of manhood.

They were good people who cared for both father and

son as long as he could remember. As they were like family to him, he was greatly relieved that he was sent to remain in Ramsgate with them instead of the great mansion that he shared with his father. But the pain of his father's loss was fresh, and he longed for his strong and kind embrace. He threw another stone into the water and brushed aside the last of his tears. He longed to swim in the pond, but ever conscientious, knew he should not return to his caregivers wet and filthy. He remembered what his father had said: to never be a nuisance and always remember that he was a Duke. Dukes simply didn't go swimming in ponds on hot summer days.

It was then that the boy heard hooves coming in his direction. He carefully moved behind a bush, ducking low in the branches so as to remain undetected. He imagined his new caregivers sent a page to retrieve him, and he did not yet wish to return to the press and cloying sympathies of the funeral attendees.

Hence, the boy was surprised to see the little girl full straddle on one of the largest horses he'd ever beheld, and wearing naught but her underthings, come crashing through the swaying willow trees that lined the pond. The Martin's only daughter was no more than eight years old, and the boy could tell it was an effort for her to swing her legs over the horse's back and slide quite a distance to reach the ground. He watched as she tied the horse's reins to a stump and was about to call out when she stepped to the pond's edge and dove fearlessly, headfirst into the water.

3

Shocked, jealous, and just a little bit concerned when she did not immediately resurface, the boy thought he should go after her. He stood up from behind the bush and quickly removed his proper morning coat and shoes. Racing to the water's edge, he gulped a lungful of air and jumped into the water, paddling with brisk strokes in the direction where the little girl dove.

The girl sputtered up out of the water just as the boy reached her. She cried out, surprised, but the alarm etched across her face quickly dissolved into good humor at her unexpected guest.

"What are *you* doing here? This is my place!"

The boy did not return her smile and, undeterred, reached for her arm. He began dragging her slowly back to the embankment as she kicked and clawed at him.

"What are you doing? Leave me alone!" she cried, "I just want to swim! What are you doing?"

The boy, older than the little sprite by several years remained calm. "I am saving you, you little fool. You shouldn't be swimming out here by yourself! Your parents will be furious with you." They reached the embankment despite the girl's protestations, and he hauled her onto the shore before doubling over, hands on his knees, to catch his breath.

The girl looked up, her blue eyes wide and pleading. "You won't tell my parents you found me here, will you? You can't tell them!" When he did not immediately respond, her tone turned angry. "You are a traitor if you do!" Sensing the boy's ire was raised she reverted to pleading. "I always come here to swim! You cannot tell—please! We can swim together!" she looked up hopefully into the boy's eyes.

The boy found himself somewhat amused by the girl's earnest face and bravery to come out so far alone by herself. But his visage remained stern as he looked upon her, nevermore so aware of his responsibilities as a duke as he observed disapprovingly the girl's unkempt hair and dirty petticoats and undershirt.

"Come," he said, averting his gaze for decorum's sake which certainly the little girl was blithely unaware. "We must get you back to your home and dried off."

"No! I will not go back! I want to swim some more!" She crossed her arms over her heaving tiny chest. The boy was now angry. "Little girl, we are going back, *now!*" He reached for her arm and dragged her unceremoniously back to her horse. He cupped his hands so she might place her foot there to mount the horse, but she refused the offer. The boy then climbed onto the horse himself and reached for her hand which she, again, refused. He looked down upon her with a regal haughtiness that belied his young age.

"Take my hand now or you will get a beating from me *and* your papa!"

The girl glared at him defiantly but saw the determination in the boy's eyes.

"I don't care if you *are* a duke! I hate you—I wish I never had to see you again! I hate that you must live here with us." She spat angrily. And though she was just a little girl, she saw his eyes flicker with hurt. The fleeting sadness now gone, he looked again upon her sternly.

"Take my hand now, or you shall reap the consequences." The girl finally grabbed the boy's forearm and, grimacing at his vice-like grip, mounted behind him.

They were met back at the stables by her panicked mamma and furious papa. Though the girl shrank under their disapproving glares, she noted disdainfully that her parents showered the boy with praise for his bravery in "rescuing" their daughter. The boy smiled and brushed off their thanks with a sigh as he walked back to the house.

The little girl watched him stride proudly away as she endured her parents' wrath. When she could stand it no more, she let loose her anger right back at them.

"Why are you not angry with *him* for leaving the grounds? Why are you only angry with *me?* It's not fair!" she cried, her face bright red as tears streamed down her cheeks.

"Gregory is a boy. And he is older than you," her father replied. The girl knew that there was no point in arguing with her father. She looked at Gregory's still retreating form with an equal mixture of disappointment and resentment. Instead of gaining a playmate as she had hoped when she was informed that the young Duke would be a ward of her parents, she was to be saddled with another jailer! Gabrielle, ever optimistic and always the adventuress, reminded herself that she was quite enterprising and, Gregory or not, would find ways to have fun despite any impediments. Indeed, finding ways to thwart the control of the haughty young duke might prove a most interesting game. At last, she smiled—a mischievous little grin of which her parents thankfully took no notice.

A RELUCTANT DEBUTANTE

*T*he moonlight crept softly through the evening mist, a pretty picture framed in the window of the girl's bedroom. With the mist, a summer breeze whispered gently, a balm against the warm night air. Like so many evenings of her youth, Gabrielle leaned as far over the windowsill as she could, gazing at the stars and the moon, savoring every breeze that helped cool her flushed cheeks. Catching another gentle breeze, she shivered pleasantly under her well-worn nightgown, as it wove through her long, golden hair.

How could she sleep when anticipation and delight beat in tandem with her heart at the thought of what awaited her come the morning? Patrice, Gabrielle's dearest friend, was to visit again and Gabrielle couldn't wait to share whispered secrets and great adventures with her closest friend. She sighed, thinking about all the wonderful dreams that had become her evening's lullaby.

Now almost 18 years old, Gabrielle thought wistfully about all the sweet summers that had passed before at the beachside town of Ramsgate. Since they were barely out of the nursery, the girls had spent their childhood summers taking turns either at Patrice's home which was next door to Ramsgate's beautiful cathedral, or at the large manse that was Gabrielle's parent's country home less than a half day's walk away, playing games, or sneaking off to their favorite swimming pond where they would strip down to their chemises and frolic unabashedly in the cool water, pretending they were exotic sea creatures. And, in truth, if anyone had stumbled upon them, they might have thought that they were indeed fairies. What a sight these two were on those dreamy endless summer days! Patrice was petite and slender, with sun-kissed chestnut hair against her dark skin, in contrast to Gabrielle, who was always tall for a girl and despite being blessed with an ample bosom, had an otherwise athletic frame that seemed meant for riding, running and vigorous exercise. Gabrielle, the fairer complected of the two, like Patrice, had long hair laying just below her slim waist as was the fashion, golden blonde streaked with platinum from the sun. Both girls had beautiful eyes that reflected the depths of their very soul. Unlike Patrice's luminous amber eyes that hinted at mystery and secrets, Gabrielle's eyes were a turquoise with silver streaks of light, and evident in their depths was her great personal strength of character and strong wit.

The girls were raised as close as any two actual sisters could be thanks to the great friendship shared by their loving parents. Gabrielle, bold and adventuress, sought exploration of the unknown, and in so doing often found herself in some mishap or other. Ramsgate and its beautiful beaches awaited them all after each winter spent in London, and there during the long summers, Gabrielle was free to run away every day with her stallion Sebastian. Flying across the great lawns of Ramsgate, and leaving the safe grounds of her home, she'd wend her way to the beaches where she remained undiscovered and undisturbed for hours. There, Gabrielle and Sebastian played in the ocean until sunset, returning home dirty but happy and always with some new story to share with her parents and their guests.

Patrice, the daughter of Ramsgate's minister, preferred to read one of her novels or banter with her friend and parents. Patrice loved gossip from London and often eavesdropped on tidings from London-town that found their way to her father's door. Gabrielle, bored by town gossip, nevertheless always indulged her friend, and together the girls laughed at their own clever imitations of London royalty and the doting Ton that swirled around them.

As they grew to teenagers, Gabrielle's long legs

enabled her to run faster and jump higher than any other girls, and most boys of her age, though such behavior, she was frequently reminded, was unbecoming a lady. When she laughed, Gabrielle did so heartily, and everyone around her was compelled to delightedly join in.

Patrice was the truly more elegant of the two, and so to her Gabrielle deferred in all things related to the London society. Gabrielle likened Patrice to a swan and herself a harpy eagle. Like the eagle, adventure filled Gabrielle's soul and unleashed her imagination.

Those magical summer days were the sweetest of their lives. Free from the constraints of London's high society, the girls explored their imaginations, unfettered by its suffocating rules of decorum.

Both were avid riders, although Patrice did not join Gabrielle in riding full saddle, together they sought adventure and new experiences. And when they were not out of doors, they immersed themselves in the prose of all the latest and greatest novelists. Gabrielle would often play-act the dramatic scenes with Patrice to the delight of the local urchins who sought them out on the sandy beaches of Ramsgate.

The girls were blissfully innocent then, content to focus on the precious moments of their last childhood summer. They did not ruminate over their future, turning an intentionally blind eye to the reality soon thrust upon all young women of a certain age. It was a future they dared not contemplate for long; should they have done so, they might have foreseen how fleeting their last summer of girlhood would be, the last spent together in such play.

The next morning Gabrielle dressed early and waited, excitedly pacing the foyer, until she finally heard the carriage wheels crackle over the long gravel driveway.

"Sally, do let me open for Patrice," Gabrielle chirped as she gently swept past the portly maid. The door swung open, and the sun poured in as Patrice bounded up the stairs to greet her open-armed hostess.

Patrice smiled brightly, a mischievous gleam in her amber eyes. "Gabrielle, I couldn't *wait* to see you today so we can plan what is destined to be 'the greatest fall event' of the season." She winked at Gabrielle, whose deep scowl creased her forehead, before bursting into peals of laughter like church bells. Patrice knew better than anyone how much Gabrielle loathed all Ton's events, but especially the ones of this season which would include her coming out into society at her eighteenth birthday ball.

Gabrielle scrunched her tiny nose and grimaced at Patrice's declaration, crossing her arms defiantly. Patrice raised her perfectly arched brows. "Tsk-tsk, very unladylike, dear Gabrielle."

"What's unladylike is how I shall scream if you take

Mama's side on that God-awful pink dress she thinks I ought to wear," Gabrielle muttered.

At that moment Dame Elizabeth Martin, Gabrielle's mother, approached the girls, long flowing skirts swishing around her. "Patrice," she sighed, taking Patrice's face in her two hands and kissing her cheeks, "Thank goodness you're here. Perhaps at last my daughter might have some sense talked into her about this birthday celebration."

Imperious and formidable always, Elizabeth Martin's shining blue eyes revealed a gentle nature. And for those closest to Elizabeth, including Patrice and her parents, Elizabeth demonstrated daily her loyalty as a friend and confidante.

"Surely, Mama, I possess all the sense I shall need in life," Gabrielle quipped. Gabrielle grimaced dramatically to her mother, sweetening it only slightly, as she reached out to clasp Patrice's hand in her own, intending to remove them from the foyer and her Mama's reach. "But never you mind that Mama, as Patrice and I have great plans for the day! I promise I will work out all the details you require for my coming out party and will do so to perfection! But please not now!" she cajoled.

Gabrielle walked ahead of Patrice, pulling her along with a smile. Elizabeth feigned mock annoyance with her daughter, hands resting daintily on her tiny hips, as she watched the girls make their escape.

Gabrielle, having temporarily secured her freedom, all demands averted for at least the time being, led the way to the great sunroom where coffee and breakfast awaited the girls. It was a beautiful summer morning and the breeze from the open veranda windows swayed the linen curtains like delicate froths of sea foam. The girls' chatting swept into the room, grabbing scones and coffee from a silver tray. Gabrielle indelicately lifted the back of her full satin skirt, and plopped herself onto a rose-colored divan, promptly flinging one leg out across the cushions. Patrice sat across from Gabrielle and chuckled as she lifted a lemon scone to her lips. "Must you be so indelicate, Gabby?"

"Oh, Patrice, you know I must find joy in life somehow. Badgering poor Mama is still at the top of the list." Gabrielle grabbed a blueberry scone and took a massive bite.

"What did you do this time to incite your Mama's displeasure? She may have smiled at me, but she certainly had more disapproving glares for you."

Gabrielle rolled her eyes. "Oh, it's this damn coming out ball! It's all Mama will discuss—yet another reason why I wish I had been born a son. I would be able to do as I please instead of being forced to play the pretty puppet for all." Gabrielle sighed as she continued, "And making matters even worse, I am quite certain Mama has ensured Lord Stalward will bring his entire entourage with him to my soiree. And you know how I have no patience for that man or his little sycophants."

Patrice listened with patient amusement as her friend

continued a merciless tirade against Lord Stalward, Gabrielle's favorite subject for complaint and annoyance. After society balls, of course.

THE ABHORRENT DUKE

*L*ord Gregory Stalward was a particularly inexplicable nuisance to Gabrielle. A fixture of the elite within London, Stalward had a devoted following of sycophants, women and men alike, all fawning over him to raise themselves in society through association with him.

"And they just grovel before him, of all baffling reasons," Gabrielle lamented to Patrice. Her friend sighed, nibbling another corner of her scone.

"You must be fair to the man," Patrice said, "The duke does not seem to actively seek London society nor its propensity to attract social climbers, wouldn't you agree? And certainly, he has taken to the responsibilities of his peerage with an admirable verve."

"I don't care if he's out delivering calves with his farmers," Gabrielle retorted, brandishing her half-eaten scone like a baton. "The fact that he neither discourages nor spurns such undeserved attention sparks my ire to no end. It is all such an abhorrent level—of conformity! How can anyone stand it?"

"Oh, my dear Gabrielle," Patrice smiled at her friend before reaching for a strawberry, "You have always snubbed your pretty nose at the antiquated. But the irony is not lost on me how opinionated you seem to be about what dress you will wear to your coming out ball- your mamma's bright pink dress not being suitable." Patrice scolded her beneath her teasing.

Gabrielle huffed. "It's not conformity. It's acceptance of the inevitable. And a choosing of my battles."

"Not the least of which will be how you handle Lord Stalward's attendance given he's such a friend of your fathers, no?" A wicked little grin pulled at the corners of Patrice's lips. She was egging Gabrielle now, and she knew it.

"You know, I shall never quite forgive London for bestowing all they have upon the esteemed Lord Stalward." Gabrielle's tone dripped sarcasm, "And yet they deny my father his due simply because he is not titled. Is he not brilliant? Is he not accomplished? That he should be regarded so little while Lord Stalward sits high atop his mighty throne is just so—" Lost for words, Gabrielle took an aggressively large bite of her scone, crumbs falling to her bosom.

"Abhorrent?" Patrice offered. Gabrielle nodded

vigorously, still chewing. And yet, Gabrielle lamented, she had been forced to endure Lord Stalward's increasing status as a fixture within the Martin's home ever since losing his father, the Duke of Montrose Edward Stalward, ten years earlier on Gregory's fourteenth birthday.

Gregory's deceased father, Lord Edward Stalward, and Gabrielle's father, Jacques Martin, had become good friends having discovered a shared interest in mathematics and science as well as similar dispositions of thoughtful, reasoned kindness and humor. When the Duke's beloved wife passed away sadly due to complications from the birth of their son Gregory, Jacques and Elizabeth welcomed both the Duke and Gregory wholeheartedly into their lives.

It was therefore not surprising that the late Lord Stalward upon his deathbed, asked Jacques to act as a guardian to Gregory until his seventeenth birthday when the boy might then resume his duties at the Stalward's residence at Montrose Estate.

It was, of course, at the Martin's home at Ramsgate that Gabrielle had her first childhood introductions to the imperious, overly sensible young Gregory. Forever in her way, the young boy delighted in foiling her machinations for childhood freedom and fun. Often, she discovered later, he was how her parents discovered her whereabouts, and she furiously called him a tattletale for months.

When Gabrielle finally recovered herself, seated across from Patrice, she smiled sweetly at her friend and simply muttered, "Indeed, he's abhorrent."

And the topic of Lord Gregory Stalward was left at that.

Across town, the very same Lord Gregory departed his London residence for a garden engagement, the first of many for the season. The coach felt hot and oppressive as it rumbled along the cobbled streets, and he squirmed uncomfortably against the trickles of sweat down his broad back. Though he found such garden parties to be quite the bore, Lord Gregory stomached them for the sake of Montrose Estate and, above all, for his father's legacy. In his breast pocket, which he patted often, were nestled two invitations: one floral invitation to today's party and another far more understated, though more amusing, missive. The latter, Gregory had been expecting to receive with some degree of excitement. It was the invitation to Gabrielle's coming out ball. He suspected Jacques Martin himself had been the one to post it, for Gabrielle would no sooner send him a letter as she would chop off all her hair. Yet he held it close nonetheless, a balm against the interminable heat of summer in the city. He sighed thinking about the cool summer breeze that would so often waft over the Martin's veranda, from the ocean's coast at Ramsgate.

To his true credit, Lord Gregory was as sensible, steadfast, and reliable as a proper duke ought to be. As his late father had but one son, Gregory was all too aware of his status as the heir of the Montrose and Stalward estate, and felt the burden of his father's death keenly. Assuming his father's mantle meant leaving behind any remaining youthful fancy. Rarely would the young duke be caught playing in the fields, nor would he laugh too loudly or be caught in any childhood antics. Indeed, he'd been quite appalled at the frivolity of young Gabrielle's existence, how she frequently arrived at dinner with soiled hems on her dresses or fresh dirt beneath her fingernails. And yet, even as a boy, he did envy her freedom, her apparent joy in everything she did.

So it was that Gregory begrudgingly came to look forward to *rescuing* the younger Gabrielle. That first summer after his father's passing, at the Martin's Ramsgate summer home, Gregory learned young Gabrielle's own routine. She would sneak out to the stables and await the moment when the stableboy took a rare break. Gabrielle would then quickly run in, mount Sebastian and off they went for another adventure.

One day soon after his arrival, fourteen-year-old Gregory had approached the Martins in the breakfast room, Gabrielle already having snuck to the stables no doubt. Gregory cleared his throat as he entered the room, interrupting the couple as Jacques seemed suspiciously close to kissing his wife, something everyone in the Martin's household were accustomed to.

Elizabeth smiled brightly at Gregory. "Good morning, Gregory! Do join us for breakfast. Sally just brought out the most delicious biscuits - and they are still warm from the oven." Elizabeth patted the seat next to her. Gregory returned her smile with a shy grin.

"Madam. Sir, I do not mean to cause you distress, but Gabrielle was just now heading towards the stables again."

Elizabeth smiled "Well, yes Gregory. She always does so after she takes her breakfast."

Reaching for a biscuit, the young duke feigned a casual tone. "And this does not worry you, Madam? She is so little to be riding and swimming alone."

Jacques and Elizabeth exchanged a private glance of amusement at their young ward's authoritative tone. Elizabeth dabbed the napkin daintily at the corners of her mouth. "Your concern for my daughter is admirable, dear boy. She is indeed a child, but even a young girl, just like a young boy, needs to explore the world a bit. The stableboy knows where she runs off to and makes certain she does not wander about too long alone before he goes after her."

Gregory's forehead furrowed a bit, and he looked down at his hands. Elizabeth rested a hand upon his shoulder and said softly, "Gregory, I think it would do you good to perhaps ride with Gabrielle. She is quite a little adventuress as you well know, and you may enjoy spending time with her."

Gregory straightened, looking up from his fingers, and spoke with all the seriousness he could muster. "Madam, my duties are such that I certainly cannot play about. I am certainly not a child like Gabrielle."

Elizabeth began to speak again when Jacques gently

placed his hand over hers, silencing her. "Lord Stalward," Jacques said, "you are correct. You are too mature to be running about as a playmate. Mrs. Martin and I understand this."

Elizabeth turned to her husband with a questioning glance. Jacques patted his mouth with his own napkin and breathed deeply before speaking again. "Lord Stalward, we have been concerned as of late with Gabrielle running about the grounds unescorted. The stable hands cannot keep up with Gabrielle, as they have their duties to fulfill naturally. And as you well know she will find a way to run off regardless of any safeguards we put in place."

Then, Jacques leaned toward Gregory. "But you, Lord Stalward, you would be able to keep up with her and make sure she does not get into any serious mischief. But to do this without her protesting, you would need to at least indulge her play within *some* reason. After all, she is just a child, whereas you are far more mature. We know that you do not approve or enjoy such frivolity given your duties, but you would be doing us quite a service."

Gregory had a feeling Elizabeth was trying to suppress a smile and there was indeed a little twinkle behind Jacques' eyes.

Jacques smiled at Elizabeth who returned his bright smile with her own wide grin. "Why yes, my husband, that is a wonderful idea! Our noble duke can help protect Gabrielle! Oh, my Lord Stalward that would be such a relief to my heart!"

Gregory looked closely at both Martins before answering with regal solemnity. "Why, certainly Sir Martin, Madam. As I am your ward, I will fulfill a duty to protect your daughter from mischief." Satisfied with the turn of the discussion, Gregory was now clearly excited and quite ready to leave the table so he could commence his new role. Gregory jumped out of his seat so quickly he almost knocked his glass off the table and then, recollecting himself, he slowly walked out of the room.

Jacques then spoke again just as Gregory laid a hand on the door. "Lord Stalward, please remember she must not realize you're there to serve as her protector. You must indulge in some of her play."

Gregory nodded, and with a bow, left the room. As soon as he closed the door behind him, he raced down the hallway as fast as his feet could carry. He did not, nor could he have imagined, the satisfied smiles that Jacques and Elizabeth Martin then shared with each other as each reached for their cups of tea.

Gregory spent three summers living with the Martins at their Ramsgate home, and when not with them, according to his deceased father the Duke's wishes, continued his academic career at Eton where all English gentlemen were schooled and readied for their future inheritances.

It had been ten years since his father had passed away, and it felt vastly longer since he assumed the mantle and responsibilities as Duke of Montrose and Stalward. Gregory, never one to allow himself to brood over things that could not be changed, felt gratitude that his father had the foresight to place him with the Martin's, under Jacques Martin's tutelage. Gregory, blessed with his father's bright and inquisitive mind, truly respected the brilliant Jaques Martin and was glad to be able to lend his name and help to the Martin's in any way he could.

The only thorn in the situation was the strong willed, rebellious Miss Gabrielle, the Martin's only daughter. Gabrielle had goaded Gregory from the start with her mischievous, carefree, and somewhat careless disposition. Gregory felt his entire summers were spent babysitting the young girl to ensure she avoided some catastrophe. And although this was a source of consternation and annoyance, if he were honest, Gregory would admit that those summers allowed him the only moments of escape from his ducal responsibilities and burdens. Gregory spent his summers *attending* to Gabrielle, swimming in the great pond and the ocean, riding, playing games of hide and seek, fishing, and climbing trees, all in the name of rescuing the "delicate" Gabrielle, of course. Gregory caught himself smiling at the thought of those three summers spent with Gabrielle in childhood play. He understood why she was somewhat disdainful of him, as she had told him often in and in no uncertain terms that she thought of him as her jailer and tattle tale. But the truth was he was grateful to her and the Martins for the respite in being ever the proper duke.

Gregory sank back in his carriage and thought about Gabrielle the woman. Now 18, she would be on the marriage market in short order. Gregory chose to dismiss the knot in his heart at the thought and instead closed his eyes and enjoyed a moment of peace.

THE LAST DAYS OF GIRLHOOD

*G*abrielle sighed, her belly full from their delicious breakfast, her thoughts turning back to the present and what was to be the last summer day of girlhood with Patrice. Gabrielle set her scone aside and walked over to the veranda window. On the grounds, the rich lawn ran like a lush carpet to the verdant tree line some hundred yards off. To the left, her mother's flower garden was in full bloom, carrying on the breeze mingled scents of hyacinth and rose. The steady *thwack* of gardener's shears trimming the topiaries blended with the effervescent hum of bees. Gabrielle's smile faded as the reality of her life broke through the pastoral scene once more.

"Oh, Patrice. Why do we need to host a ball anyway? Why waste the last days of our summer planning this dreadful event? It rings like a death knell every time my thoughts chance upon it! I'd much prefer to go down to the stables, saddle the horses, and ride down to the shore."

Gabrielle turned and raced to her friend's side, grabbing Patrice's hands between hers pleadingly. "Soon we will both be confined to London society, our movements noted constantly, watched by everyone and especially by that dreadful matchmaking witch, Lady Deville. So, please, can we not just forget everything else today and just *play*?" Gabrielle's stormy eyes were mischievous and emphatic. Patrice knew this look well.

Patrice stood, grinning at her friend. "Very well, my dear Gabrielle. Let's have at it, only on one condition." Patrice raised her finger pointedly to Gabrielle before she continued, "Tonight you will finalize your menu with your Mama and help me with my gown selection." Patrice extended her bronzed fingers, offering her hand to her friend in truce and promise. "Gentlemen's honor Gabrielle?"

Gabrielle huffed, brushing her hair away from her furrowed brow, ample bosom rising as she sighed. Gabrielle raised her hand in response. "Oh, all right. Gentlemen's honor." The two friends shook hands and rushed off to the stables to fetch their horses.

It never failed Gabrielle's notice that her family estate at Ramsgate was the most magical place to be in the summer. Far outside the reaches of London, Ramsgate offered unfettered beauty and close access to the glorious beaches of east Kent. The Martins always kept a summer place, having met there in their youth on its sandy shores. As Gabrielle and Patrice arrived at the stables, the sun peeked its warm face between the clouds, casting full beams of light in their path as they saddled their horses and set off. They hardly needed to guide the horses as the faint smell of seaweed and salt wafted closer and closer, spurring they're mounts on a joyous gallop. So caught in the wind, the girl's hair was gently pulled from their careful braids to stream loose behind them. It felt, Gabrielle thought, like freedom.

The young women enjoyed the day for all its worth. They rested on the sandy shores, flicked their toes in the lapping waves, let the sun bring forth freckles on their cheeks, and, having spent hours riding the beautiful stallions up and down the beaches of Ramsgate, they played and danced in the waves. It truly was, Gabrielle thought, the best way to cherish these last days of summer. Finally, as the sun settled its fiery brilliance on the horizon, Gabrielle stretched her arms over her head and reluctantly stood.

"The horses need to eat and drink," she sighed, "let's head back."

"Thank you for today," Patrice said as she, too, stood. Gabrielle nodded, refusing to let the little knot of sadness in her stomach resurface after their pristine day. The girls walked for quite some time in silence, heading back from the beach towards the great lawn of the Martin's estate. Gabrielle could not help but feel a bit despondent at the thought that this might be their last truly free day to be girls and not young women.

"Patrice?" Gabrielle asked after a time, "Will we never again enjoy these days of summer?" Gabrielle turned to hide a tear, knowing that she sounded childish and melodramatic.

"Oh, Gabrielle," Patrice said, clasping her friend's hand, "Surely life does not work in such absolutes. Things will change, yes, but we mustn't give up hope that such fun will vanish forever."

"Do you promise?"

"As much as I can, yes." Patrice squeezed Gabrielle's hand and the two young women fell into companionable silence once more.

Regardless of Gabrielle's independent nature, she knew that she must try to fulfill the expectations of her parents and society. Nonetheless, Gabrielle looked upon any impending marriage proposal with dread. She knew her Mama was already concerned that her daughter would not make every effort to seek a suitable match when the time came. Her thoughts must have been more visible across her normally bright features because Patrice spoke again.

"Gabrielle, you will always be a free spirit. Even when you're married. Look at our mothers—they both enjoy their marriages and neither feel compromised," Patrice continued. "You will find your perfect mate. I know that we both will."

Gabrielle sighed. "I wish I shared your certainty, Patrice. I have seen the fops that abound. They are silly boys, sometimes more delicate than many of the women, certainly me. You, on the other hand, are elegant and regal and will find someone who will value that. But perhaps," Gabrielle laughed, "just maybe I will frighten away the majority of suitors. That might be just the thing I need to do!"

"You are being ridiculous Gabrielle," Patrice protested. "You are stunning, and you will have every young man attending to your every movement at your debut. And as for me? Candidly, I cannot wait for my own debut!"

Patrice's own debut was scheduled only weeks after Gabrielle's. Unlike Gabrielle, Patrice looked forward to meeting a young man, which still baffled Gabrielle though far be it for her to trample her friend's excitement.

"Gabrielle," Patrice continued animatedly, "You will find someone you admire and respect. I am certain of it. But you owe it to yourself, and your family, at the very least to be open to trying. I know you will be dutiful and marry but why not also try and find someone you truly esteem? You deserve to try Gabrielle. Marriage is a duty that neither of us can avoid."

Gabrielle stifled a shudder as Patrice went on. "You are the only child of your family, as am I, which means that if we do not marry, our family lines end with us. And setting that aside, beyond any duty to our family, don't you ever think about the joy of one day having your own family and raising your own children if we are so blessed?"

Gabrielle shrugged but made no reply. She remained silent as she and Patrice arrived back to the stables, lost in thinking what her future might bring.

A YOUNG LADY'S PLACE IN SOCIETY

*T*he girls ran upstairs to their rooms so they could quickly wash and change before dinner. Gabrielle deliberately took longer, out of spite, having heard the servants tittering that Lord Stalward would be in attendance.

Since the esteemed lord came of age and left Ramsgate for his family estate, Gabrielle fortunately had little direct contact with him unless it was in her father's workroom. She could hardly recollect the childhood playmate he'd been—or at least had pretended to be. It was true that for a while Lord Gregory had seemed to cast off the severity of his rank to indulge in moments of childhood with her, accompanying her to the pond at Ramsgate and for many a high-speed gallop through the fields. But she distinctly remembered the day it all changed.

She'd been nearly ten years old, clever, and well-accustomed to sneaking down the stairs unnoticed. She'd been ready to dart in front of the entryway to the sitting room, the door of which was ajar, when she heard voices: both of her parents and, to her surprise, Lord Gregory. On silent slippers, she crept closer and overheard with growing fury that they spoke of her.

"…She seems to have no regard for any decorum," Lord Gregory had intoned in a perfectly condescending teenaged drawl.

"We certainly do appreciate your concern for Gabrielle's modesty," her Mama replied. Gabrielle could hear the smile behind her mother's words but was too distracted to question it.

"And her language!" Lord Gregory said, "Really, madam, I'm not sure where such a child would learn vulgarities, but her tongue is as sharp as a razor."

"Well," her father spoke, "It is possible the attendants in my workshop have little sense of modesty around such impressionable girls."

"I should say so," Gregory replied. Behind the door, Gabrielle clenched her fingers into fists. *How dare he!* Surely any friend of hers would never say such things! *Because he never was your friend*, she thought. *He was just a spy. A tattle.* For reasons she couldn't quite place,

Gabrielle felt sadness pool in her gut. She was so distracted by this revelation, that she almost missed the next words to fall from her father's mouth.

"Why don't you accompany Gabrielle and me to the workshop from time to time?" her father said. In the shadows, Gabrielle nearly gasped in indignation. Her father's workshop—the only space she had where she might shed her feminine mantle and be treated like the intelligent person she was—and *he* was going to be there? Policing her every move, every word? Not only would Lord Gregory be there, but that it was at her father's behest stung far more than anything. No, Gabrielle could not bear it. She fled from the doorway, tears stinging her eyes, as Lord Gregory's response to the affirmative chased her.

And so, it had been for the next seven summers that Lord Gregory accompanied Gabrielle nearly everywhere. Gone was her playmate and in his stead was an imperious, oppressive young man bent on criticizing her every word. Her father's workshop, where he was breaking ground on London's newest waterworks project, had been the worst of it.

Jacques Martin's ingenious system made Gabrielle exceedingly proud of her father: a sewage system that would revolutionize the city and, if predictions were to be believed, virtually eliminate the deadly summer cholera outbreaks. Where Gabrielle had previously been allowed a seat at her father's table, she increasingly found herself shouldered out by Lord Gregory who, she suspected, only feigned interest in her father's projects for the sole purpose of being an annoyance to her. Worse still was the obvious regard that her father had for the young Duke. Lord Gregory exhibited his deceased father's intellectual talent and now fostered under the tutelage of Jacques Martin, Lord Gregory indeed was a formidable engineer and scientist, a true partner with her father in his scientific efforts. It was therefore that instead of looking forward to summers with Lord Gregory, her teenage years found her looking forward to his departure more than anything for only then was she allowed her rightful seat next to her father where her ideas might be shared, and her opinion might be valued.

When Gabrielle finally deigned to grace the dining hall with her presence, sweeping into the dining room with as haughty air as she could manage, Patrice was already seated next to Lord Gregory. Her father sat, as was customary, at the head of the table with her mother at the opposite end. Lord Gregory sat to her father's right, and since Patrice was already seated next to him, that left the only open chair for Gabrielle to her father's left and directly across from Lord Gregory for the whole evening. Gabrielle wasn't sure which was worse: being next to the man's elbow or having to stare at his face all evening.

He glanced at Gabrielle, his sharp eyes meeting her own in quiet appraisal, before tilting his head informally and turning his attention back to the table.

"Father, how was your day in London?" Gabrielle asked, breezing to her seat, "Any news of the final launch of the waterworks system?" She reached for a buttered roll and took a big bite. Jacques smiled, always pleased at his inquisitive daughter's interest in his work.

He dabbed his napkin at the side of his mouth before answering her, "The system is officially being implemented throughout London. We must now be patient and ensure that the infrastructure we designed will be as successful as we hoped."

"Jacques, your designs are impeccable," Lord Gregory interjected, "Based on our latest drawings, there can be nothing to fear—you are a genius."

Gabrielle darted a piercing glance at Lord Gregory. *She* had not been permitted to see the latest plans, and Gregory knew it. Underneath the table, Gabrielle's white-gloved fingers curled into fists.

Jacques raised his wine glass to Gregory, sincerely returning the compliment. "My dear Gregory, these are *our* collective designs. Your work, and that of our friend Lord James Rittenhouse, and of course you too, Gabrielle," Jacques placated having seen his daughter's steadily seething gaze, "Have all contributed to the success of this water system making our dream into a reality. Never forget that. Your father would be very proud of you Gregory, just as I am of you… and Gabrielle."

Gabrielle relaxed slightly at her father's words. Lord Gregory may not recognize her intellectual value, but her father always would. She smiled as Lord Gregory raised his eyebrow at Jacques' mention of Gabrielle as a contributor but smiled back before changing the subject.

Patrice and Gabrielle's mother Elizabeth smiled at one another content, that Jacques Martin had been able to diffuse his daughter's wrath so easily. The women whispered to one another behind their napkins, likely something to do with the upcoming ball, but Gabrielle was quickly distracted when she overheard Lord Gregory whisper to her father.

"Jacques, we must speak about Norwood." He reached forward and speared a roasted potato with his knife. "I have some concerns that we need to discuss"

Jacques raised his hand, interrupting Lord Gregory mid-sentence, and quietly responded, casting a glance in the direction of Patrice, whose uncle was the same man in question. "Please, not tonight, and not at the dinner table. This dinner is to be a celebration of my daughter, and Patrice. I would request that any business talk be saved for a more somber occasion." Lord Gregory picking up on the hint, nodded smiling, and raised his crystal wine glass to his lips.

Gabrielle eager to hear any news related to the waterworks project was sensitive to pursue any discussion regarding Norwood in front of her dear friend Patrice. But she made a note to ask her father about this when they were alone.

Alfred Norwood had been a small, annoying thorn to the Martin family and the whole waterworks project since its inception, but Jacques firmly changed the subject to more sociable matters. "Tonight," he said, "we must hear all the details of Gabrielle's coming out party. Have you ladies made any progress on the planning?"

Gabrielle crossed her arms at her bosom and leaned away from the table, objecting to the change in direction her father proposed. "Why on earth do we need to discuss this silly party when we all would much prefer to hear about your project, Papa?" Lord Gregory smiled "Well, I for one would be delighted to hear your plans,Gabrielle. You will be introduced formally into society and have to join the rest of us in enduring the necessary proprieties. Let's raise a toast to both our debutantes, Gabrielle and Patrice" Gabrielle's cheeks flamed a pretty hot pink as she met his gaze suspecting that he was teasing her. As she raised her glass to her lips she noticed the Duke's eyes become hooded and fixed... on her lips. Flustered, Gabrielle was grateful that Patrice had broken the spell of the moment. "Oh, Gabrielle, your ball will be so wonderful," Patrice chimed in.

"Gabrielle, please show some patience for goodness' sake. We have worked so hard on your debut! The flowers are arranged, the entertainment called, the invitations sent.

It will be a tremendous success so long as you show up and make some small attempt to actually enjoy yourself!" Elizabeth teased, smiling at her daughter indulgently.

Gabrielle bristled but managed to smile thinly back at her Mama. "Mother I will certainly attempt to do both. But I would much rather work alongside Papa if only I were permitted!"

"Women ought not to trouble themselves with the filth and tedium of sewers and waterways," Lord Gregory scoffed.

"And would you also, then, Lord Gregory, prefer that women not trouble themselves with their children when they are ill or worse, *dying* of cholera? For it seems that whether mothers are dealing with their infants' loose bowels in the home or when it runs down the street to infect more babies, women are as much involved in the safety of our sewers as the men!"

Lord Gregory reddened at the topic of raw sewage, Gabrielle so cavalierly threw about the dinner table, and Gabrielle grinned truly for the first time that evening at his discomfort.

Elizabeth smiled brightly, talking a little too loudly and cheerfully to change the subject. Turning to Patrice, she said, "Well, I do believe that Gabrielle said she would endeavor to enjoy herself. Isn't that the most positive comment I have heard from Gabrielle since we started the planning? Progress is being made! Patrice, I do believe we owe this to you talking some sense to your friend."

Patrice laughed, jolting out of the way as Gabrielle attempted to kick her friend under the table. "No, Ma'am, I would never dare take credit for any of Gabrielle's thoughts or opinions." Patrice smiled back at her hostess and avoided Gabrielle's annoyed gaze.

"Smart young lady, Miss Patrice, particularly since so many of those ideas are somewhat flawed," interjected Lord Gregory with a sardonic smile.

Gabrielle glared at him across the table. She resented Lord Gregory's teasing, particularly as he was able to freely work in any way that he chose, and alongside her Papa, while Gabrielle had only her debut ball to look forward to —her mind longed for more challenge.

"I would be curious to know, Lord Gregory, which of my ideas you deem so flawed?"

Lord Gregory stiffened in his seat, but Elizabeth leaned forward and took Gabrielle's hand patting it lightly. "Now, now. Gregory did not mean anything by his teasing. Did you Gregory?" Elizabeth raised a delicate eyebrow, making it impossible for him to argue with her.

"Why, no, Ma'am not at all," Gregory smoothly replied. He relaxed in his seat, but when Gabrielle caught his gaze, she noted that a corner of the man's infuriating mouth twitched into the barest hint of a smile.

Elizabeth smiled and then proceeded to launch seamlessly into the endless details of the debut ball, everything from the menu to the flower arrangements and number of guests.

Gregory glanced at Gabrielle who was brooding as she played with her food. Feeling his gaze upon her, Gabrielle lifted her own. He winked at her and before she could stop it, she felt color rising in her cheeks which just made the aggravating man grin more.

CELEBRATION AND REPROACH

*A*s the last days of summer trailed long behind them, the Martins, along with many London families in the Ton, returned to their homes in the city for the start of the season in early September. Jacques and Lord Gregory met daily as the extensive plans for the waterworks system were implemented by teams of men under the supervision of Lord James Rittenhouse, Lord Gregory's schoolmate and closest friend. Jacques and Gregory usually met at the Martin's residence, as they finalized their parts and troubleshooted any unforeseen impediments. Thankfully, with many of the meetings occurring in her father's study, Gabrielle was able to include herself in their discussions much, she gleefully noted, to Lord Gregory's chagrin. She noticed, though, that even he begrudgingly admitted when she'd made a fair or logical point regarding this juncture or that. It was reward enough for Gabrielle to thwart the man's arrogance and she grinned brilliantly, sweetly, at him all the while.

One late night, Gabrielle happened upon her father and Lord Gregory in a heated debate. She strode into her father's study, intent on learning the cause of the tiff.

"Surely you must see," her Papa asserted, "how the safety seals here and certainly at Charing's Cross must be serviced by human hands! They are simply at too large a pinch-point to go unattended!"

"And I'd hoped you'd see, good sir, that human error is too great a risk for these points. They must be fully automated and regulated by machines. We *must* trust in the automation of the future, Jacques! Men will never be able to keep up with these as needed."

"We cannot so blindly put our faith in machines!" Jacques insisted.

"They are machines designed by us and to trust in them means to trust our ingenuity," Lord Gregory countered. And so the two went on as Gabrielle listened until at last she chimed in.

"I think," she said, her voice carrying high above the two agitated men, "That Lord Gregory is correct."

Silence descended over the room rapidly. "I beg your pardon?" Lord Gregory said, bemused. Gabrielle sighed. *This would certainly go to the man's head.* But she moved to the right side of the study where a large chalkboard dominated the wall. In several succinct equations, she proved the effectiveness of Lord Gregory's ideas, how it would save in both manpower and long-term maintenance costs at key junctures of the water pipes.

Lord Gregory snorted, amused, as Jacques cleared his throat. "Well, Gabrielle," her Papa said, "I must say you have proven Gregory's point succinctly. Excellent work … both of you."

Gabrielle smiled, hands on her hips until her eyes met Lord Gregory's once more. His expression was … unsettling, she decided, a mixture of admiration and something deeper she couldn't quite place. A knot squeezed in her stomach as she beheld the warmth in his eyes, and she couldn't help but smile at him in turn. He tipped his head in thanks, his lips curling pleasantly, and suddenly the knot in her gut unfurled with a burst of electricity crashing through Gabrielle from the top of her head down to her toes, pooling hotly deep in her core. She flushed, placing a hand upon her bosom.

Gregory was the first to break the spell, turning abruptly to walk over to the desk to begin work on the automation. Gabrielle, not as easily able to compose herself, excused herself to fetch some water. Outside the door of the study, she leaned against the corridor wall and sighed deeply. Gradually, her heart's rhythm slowed, the flush in her cheeks sliding back to her normal complexion.

The week before Gabrielle's great debut ball, Lord Gregory rushed to the Martin's home late one evening without announcing himself, barging into the quiet study where Gabrielle and Jacques were heads-together over ductwork plans. While it was not unusual for Lord Gregory to stop by unannounced, one look at his flustered face had both Jacques and Gabrielle rounding the table to offer him a seat.

"What is it, Gregory?" Jacques inquired as he reached for the brandy he always kept well stocked on the mantle.

"Jacques, we must speak…alone," Gregory replied, glancing dismissively at Gabrielle.

"Need I remind you that this is my home, *Lord* Stalward," Gabrielle snapped. "I most certainly will not remove myself at your behest within the walls of my own house." Gabrielle crossed her arms.

Jacques turned to her after a moment, reading a deeper concern in Lord Gregory that Gabrielle could not divine. "Please, my dear," Jacques spoke softly, "leave us. All will be well."

"But father—" Gabrielle's disappointment was evident.

Jacques looked at his daughter with soft reproach and Gabrielle let her protests die on her lips. Her father would not be moved this time. With that, Gabrielle lifted her head high and swept past Lord Gregory, tossing him a look of disgust and anger.

Just outside the door, she leaned against the wall, straining her ears to catch snippets of the ensuing conversation. The only thing she could distinguish was the name Norwood, which Gabrielle knew was never a good omen given his history. Lord Norwood, a gloomy and unsavory presence in London society, had also put in a bid for the construction of the waterworks system, believing no doubt, that his rank would all but ensure his position as the man who'd revolutionize London. When it was decided that Jacques Martin would lead the project, an untitled and invariably lower-class family than Norwood, the man had very nearly declared open vengeance upon the Martin family. Jacques, basking in the accolades of his initial design, thought little of Lord Norwood's threats. Titles were not everything to Jacques Martin, who'd no doubt won the favor of the contract based purely on his altruistic nature and the value he placed on ensuring safety and cleanliness for everyone, rich or poor.

Gabrielle only heard Lord Norwood's name uttered furtively from within her father's study, but not the context of Lord Gregory's obvious concern when he happened upon them. With a frustrated huff, she pushed off the wall and retreated to her room.

Gabrielle was burning with curiosity. What had been so important that her father would dismiss her so willingly? And what on earth would have caused the panic she'd witnessed in Lord Gregory's visage? Surely, Lord Norwood had not found a way to sabotage her Papa's projects? Sleep eluded her for some time afterward as she churned over the possibilities in her mind, each more disastrous than the last, particularly because Lord Norwood featured in all of them.

The week of Gabrielle's debut ball felt like a month, as the only distraction in the Martin household was the plans for Gabrielle's ball. At last, the long-awaited evening was upon them.

Gabrielle had been coiffed, perfumed, and dressed with the greatest care. She wore her mother's diamond necklace and earrings, gifts from her grandparents at her birth. Her blonde hair, intricately braided and wrapped into a crown atop her head, glistened as brightly as the jewels she wore. Gabrielle permitted to select her own gown and fabric, had decided on a satin pink champagne gown with small hints of matching lace around the cap sleeves and bodice. The dress fit her statuesque body perfectly and she had to admit she enjoyed the way it lifted her bosom ever so slightly, accentuating her curves. As a last touch, she pulled on white gloves that ended just above her elbows.

Elizabeth's parents, the Baron and Baroness Reynolds, had happily lent their London mansion to the Martins' for their granddaughter Gabrielle's coming out party. The mansion had an enormous ballroom, bedecked in wall-to-wall gilded mirrors set below rich forest scene tapestries. Gold sconces adorned every wall, casting a soft glow to all corners of the ballroom. Above the gleaming dance floor, four crystal chandeliers lit the ballroom with bright fractures of light.

Most of the guests had already arrived when Gabrielle made her way to the grand staircase to be announced. The crowd stilled as she stepped forward, bracing her hands on the polished wooden banisters. Butterflies swirled unexpectedly in her stomach, and she heard her name announced as if from a great distance. Taking a steadying breath, Gabrielle slowly descended the staircase, feeling all eyes on her. She smiled brightly at last, as her eyes fell on Patrice. She sensed many of the young men of London had their keen eyes trained on her and, although she was aware that she was considered rather pretty, she realized in that moment that their gazes were more than just admiring. They were … lustful. Predictably, the crowd of young men trailed her as Gabrielle moved across the ballroom to greet her friend. Patrice clasped Gabrielle's hands in her gloved ones, positively beaming.

"Well, there is no turning back now, is there?" Gabrielle whispered to Patrice who giggled with a shake of her head in response.

"You look stunning, Gabrielle," Patrice said before flicking a quick glance over Gabrielle's shoulder. "And it seems apparent that all of London's bachelors agree, too," she said with a sly smile.

"Come," Gabrielle said, looping her arm through Patrice's, "Walk with me. For we must fortify ourselves against the amassing hordes."

Gabrielle had to admit the ball was a complete resounding success. The champagne flowed, the musicians kept up a ceaseless repertoire, and light chatter diffused through the perfumed air. No detail or finery was spared to mark this the event of the season. If it had ended at that, Gabrielle might not have minded the dance after all. However, the moment she and Patrice made their way back across the ballroom, both women were accosted by eager fops desperate for a dance.

Before Gabrielle had even made it to the champagne flutes, her dance card was full. She did her best to smile warmly at each man, no doubt each one someone her parents would view as a potential suitor. She took a turn with the young Duke of Cambridge, barely a year older than she and who, she was shocked to see, wore hints of makeup. Then there was the heir to the earl of some estate in Sussex, who whispered almost as if he was afraid to be overheard by anyone, including herself. Gabrielle spent the dance asking him to speak up. Followed by him was the Duke of Norfolk, whose conversation focused solely on the size of his land, the number of tenants he cared for, and the last count of sheep herds. Gabrielle stifled her obvious relief when yet another gentry boy tapped the Duke's shoulder and he had no choice but to nervously oblige. Her new partner, an earl from Bedford, looked at her as if she were a trifle dessert on display, even going so far as to lick his lips lasciviously. Gabrielle's stomach twisted. It was at that moment she caught site of Patrice swirling on the dance floor.

Patrice was dancing just short of scandalously close, with the son of the most powerful landlord of the London gentry: the first-born Lord James Rittenhouse. Gabrielle's jaw nearly hit the floor.

James was tall and lean, with jet black hair, and icy blue eyes. His mistresses were stories of legend in London society; enigmatic and captivating, they were actresses, opera singers, and ballet dancers. Indeed, there seemed so many mistresses to his name, that many felt he would never marry let alone pursue anyone in society eligible for marriage. Lord Rittenhouse's romantic life was in complete contrast to his work and demeanor within London, where he dutifully upheld responsibilities as the only son of the great Rittenhouse lineage. James was also actively involved in London's waterworks renewal and a trusted friend of both Lord Gregory and Jacques Martin. It was said that his mother had been notoriously unfaithful to her doting elderly husband and that she died of syphilis. Perhaps, Gabrielle mused, it was this that fostered James' innate spurning of the institution of marriage.

Just beyond Patrice and James, Gabrielle glimpsed another figure in the crowd. One last twirl with her odious dance partner and she further glimpsed the somber Lord Gregory Stalward, Duke of Montrose. It was no surprise that he lurked so near James Rittenhouse as the two were peas in an irritating pod, Gabrielle thought.

Lord Gregory's attention seemed focused upon Patrice and James, but as soon as Gabrielle's gaze set upon him, Lord Gregory's dark eyes found Gabrielle's and he raised his glass to her, his smile sly and his gaze steady. A shiver bolted pleasantly down her spine, though Gabrielle turned away from Lord Gregory and back to Patrice as the handsome Lord James twirled her around the dance floor, her sapphire gown shimmering in the candlelight. Gabrielle's brow furrowed as she reflected on this scene, still dancing about the ballroom with her partner who seemed oblivious to Gabrielle's distractedness. *What might Lord Rittenhouse want with dear Patrice?* Gabrielle thought. Surely Patrice would not succumb to anything untoward from the infamous playboy, but men, she knew, could be charming and odious all at the same time. As the dance mercifully ended, she found her gaze settled once more upon Lord Gregory.

Gabrielle's thoughts were abruptly interrupted by an unwelcome, shrill voice. "My *dearest* Gabrielle, what congratulations to you!"

Gabrielle turned, a smile already plastered across her face. "Lady Deville. To what do I owe such wonderful congratulations?"

Lady Deville, her peacock fan fluttering imperiously before her face, grasped Gabrielle's arm tightly with her free hand. Lady Deville was London's staple gossip, matchmaker, and general purveyor of all that was acceptable and proper within their tight-knit society. If one were to know of anything scandalous or otherwise noteworthy, surely it came from Lady Deville's thin, red lips. Tonight the woman was bedecked in a rather gaudy shade of purple, her rouge and powder so caked onto her aging face that the lines around her gleeful mouth were even more pronounced.

"Oh, my dear," she droned, "So *coy!*" Lady Deville steered her behind a column to speak with her privately. "Gabrielle, I have just heard the marvelous news that Lord Stalward has made an offer of marriage to *you!* And of course, you have accepted!"

INSULT TO INJURY

*I*t felt, for a moment, as if Gabrielle's heart stopped beating. A coldness washed over her as Lady Deville grinned a toothy grin, waiting for her response. After a beat, Gabrielle drew herself to her full height and met Lady Deville's eager gaze with equanimity, despite the fast beat of her heart. "Madame Deville. I can say with absolute certainty that I am not engaged with anyone. I'd thank you for not encouraging such fallacious rumors. Please do enjoy the rest of your evening."

Gabrielle made a move to leave, but Lady Deville still had hold of her arm and clamped down more firmly with her beefy, surprisingly strong, hands. "Not so fast, Miss Martin," she hissed, "Have you no concern for your family name? The honor with which such a match will help not just yourself but your parents? Has your mother taught you nothing about the foolishness of flying where you may in the face of society?"

Gabrielle twisted her arm from the woman's grasp, but Lady Deville continued undeterred. "You were always a headstrong and difficult child, Gabrielle, but I did not think you selfish. Think! Think of what you will be doing if you reject Lord Stalward. He is a good man and such a reckless rebuff would not ruin just you! Your foolish and hasty decision will ruin your entire family."

Gabrielle felt a cold sweat beading on her forehead but she persisted in as measured a tone as she could muster. "Lady Deville, I must beg that you importune me no more with rumors and innuendo. This is a matter that has nothing to do with you, and I assure you that your advice is unnecessary. I am not betrothed, nor have been asked to wed anyone! Now please I ask that you let me and this distasteful subject pass. I bid you *adieu*."

Gabrielle swiftly made a beeline for the veranda, to the fresh air and quiet, passing Patrice still on the dance floor in Lord James' arms. As the girls' eyes met, Patrice's brow furrowed with concern, but Gabrielle smiled and made a show of fanning herself as if she had overheated before hurrying on.

Outside, the fountains of the Reynolds Castle burbled merrily in the gardens, the edges of which were visible to Gabrielle as she leaned against the railing on the veranda, taking in deep gulps of the crisp evening air. Her blood boiled in anger and anxiousness over her confrontation with the formidable Lady Deville. How would such a rumor have come to pass, anyhow? But furthermore, how dare Lady Deville assume to approach Gabrielle about such a matter?

The mere idea of Lord Gregory bending a knee to propose to her was preposterous. Though he was a dear friend to her father, he'd never expressed one iota of interest in Gabrielle as a person, much less a young woman. Lord Stalward had long seemed to have returned some of the antipathy toward Gabrielle that she felt for him.

More recently, Gabrielle reflected, anytime she and her family were visited by Lord Stalward, he quickly found some excuse or other to leave the room, especially on the rare occasion he was left alone with Gabrielle. Gabrielle didn't know what to make of it, nor did Patrice with whom Lord Stalward did seem to hold some affection, as he would converse more freely with her.

Gabrielle hugged herself as she thought about what her future held with a rumor of this magnitude over her. Although not ready for marriage despite the attentions of tonight's ball, Gabrielle knew marriage with someone was inevitable. And now having marked her eighteenth birthday, there was no escaping the fact that she would be on the marriage market in short order.

"Lord Stalward propose to *me*?" Gabrielle mused aloud, "As if that were even remotely possible." Gabrielle laughed at the absurdity of the notion. A family friend or not, Lord

Gregory Stalward was the furthest possibility for a suitor that Gabrielle could conceive.

The idea, though completely unreasonable, could not help but conjure the man and his strong visage to her mind. There was no denying that Lord Gregory was no "butter boy," as Patrice and Gabrielle were fond of calling the many soft, milky white fops of London. He'd always cut a tall and imposing figure, broad shouldered and broad chested, with hair the color of a lion's mane. His sly smile was quick and his blue eyes keen and sharp. Gabrielle always thought he looked more roguish than any Lord of Montrose. Though even she had to admit, where she once thought this a flaw in his appearance, she couldn't help now think of the way his lips curled when he looked at her or the way the amused arc of his eyebrows sent a little shiver racing through her. It was, she determined, entirely vexing.

As if summoned by her own unruly thoughts, Gabrielle suddenly heard footsteps approaching behind her. She turned and met the bold gaze of the very man himself whose thoughts created this tumultuous anxiety in her breast. He strode across the veranda, removing his jacket as Gabrielle remained rooted to her place on the balcony. Without waiting for a comment, he swung his jacket across her shoulders, the warmth of it settling across her arms as his hands rested on her shoulders for a moment.

Regaining her composure, Gabrielle scoffed, "Well, if being alone with you on the veranda doesn't illicit some gossip, Lord Gregory, my wearing your jacket certainly will."

Lord Gregory dropped his hands from her shoulders and, though he still stood close, Gabrielle immediately felt strangely chilled. His eyes held hers for a moment before he spoke. "I couldn't help but notice that you were subject to the attentions of society's most avid matchmaker. I feared Lady Deville may have been the cause of some distress."

Gabrielle, stunned by Lord Gregory's imposing presence and that he admitted he followed her onto the quiet terrace intentionally, struggled for a reply. "Never you fear, Lord Gregory. Lady Deville thinks highly of her own importance, an outlook that I dare say it vexes her that I do not share. She could no more cause me distress than a common field mouse."

Lord Gregory stifled a chuckle. "I hear that even field mice often cause distress for most young women."

"I, Lord Gregory, am not 'most young women,'" Gabrielle replied defiantly, lifting her chin toward him. Her breath stole from her lungs, however, when Lord Gregory took another step towards her, closing the distance between them to something near scandalous. He was close enough that she could see he had flecks of gold in his otherwise blue eyes, close enough to smell the pomade in his hair and the sweet wine on his breath, close enough that if she leaned forward, only a little, her bosom might brush the broad plane of his chest.

Lord Gregory raised a hand, hesitantly at first, but then with more confidence. A flush rose to Gabrielle's cheeks and a strange heat pooled low in her stomach. Time sputtered to a halt as Lord Gregory slowly, agonizingly slowly, trailed his thumb along her jawline. His touch was feather-light, surprisingly gentle, and Gabrielle was astonished, both at his forwardness and how much she suddenly yearned to lean into the touch, to make it more forceful and concrete.

"No," he murmured, "you are not like most women." His eyes remained locked with Gabrielle's, their breath swirling between them in the chilled air.

Gabrielle broke his stare first, flicking her attention for the briefest moments to his parted lips before she summoned a deep breath and responded, "Ah, well since your intuition is so sharp, Lord Stalward, you will understand why I ask that you do not engage me in any more unpleasant or frivolous conversation this evening."

In one movement, Gabrielle removed the jacket, handing it back to Lord Gregory, as she stepped away from him and moved back toward the glittering ballroom.

"What is your hurry, Gabrielle? I wish to speak with you." Gregory's voice was typically commanding but now also with a seductive undercurrent that Gabrielle had never experienced from him before. Her skin pricked with goosebumps.

Gabrielle held her head high and turned to face him despite her pounding heart. "Lord Stalward, your wish to speak with me tonight is not only surprising, but truly strange indeed. We are in one another's company regularly with my parents. There are many moments enough for you to find and speak with me rather than here, now, and this evening, on this veranda, when I am unchaperoned, no less. I am leaving and ask that you do not follow me! The gossips will have a field day with this as you well must know."

She was almost back inside, the conversation in the ballroom buzzing in the air like a beehive, when Gabrielle was able to catch his last whispered words. The words stopped her cold. "Gabrielle, I will call on you tomorrow."

She looked back over her shoulder, his voice sending a shiver down her spine, his eyes intense and gleaming. Her breath caught in her throat for a moment before she steeled herself and turned away from the man once more.

As Gabrielle stepped back into the warmth of the ballroom, Patrice swept over, clasping her hands, cheeks rosy from the dance and excitement. "Gabrielle, my dear, you must dance! I know the butter boys are all out in abundance this evening, but there are some handsome men here as well."

Gabrielle smiled tightly, turning her attention away from what had just transpired on the veranda, and in hushed tones whispered, "Patrice, Lord Rittenhouse may be handsome but his reputation is dangerous, wouldn't you agree? Careful there."

Patrice rolled her eyes, shrugging her shoulders. "Don't

be ridiculous— James is merely a family friend and you know that. He is no different than Lord Stalward, who I did happen to notice, along with the rest of the ballroom, found you on the terrace." She wiggled her eyebrows. "What on earth was all that about?"

"Absolutely nothing worth talking about," Gabrielle responded with a nervous giggle and then more loudly, "Now can we please get some punch, and then I shall dance the night away!"

One of the young men, overhearing this last part, ran to get Gabrielle a punch as Jacques swept to her side, gallantly offered his hand, and led her to the dance floor.

The remainder of the evening, Gabrielle and Patrice managed to take a turn with every eligible young man save the brooding Lord Gregory Stalward, who danced with no one at all, despite many longing glances cast by the single women in attendance. All evening, Lord Gregory chose instead to lean against a column, dismissing most conversation except with Lord James Rittenhouse and Gabrielle's father.

Much to her dismay, however, Gabrielle noticed that his eyes moved over her all evening long. She was perplexed, too, that no matter how many young men she danced with, she couldn't seem to shake the feeling of Lord Gregory's touch down her face, the lingering heat it left. She dismissed the traitorous thoughts as much as possible from her mind as she took another turn on the dance floor with yet another butter boy.

A PROPOSAL MADE

A week after her London debut Gabrielle was relieved to awaken back in her very own sunny room at Ramsgate. They'd only arrived back the day prior, but already she'd spent the afternoon since arriving home along the beach, trying to clear her mind from the tumultuous thoughts. This last week she had been dealt the full force of London's gossip. All because of Lord Stalward and his forging ahead with a plan which, once revealed to her, made her feel ever the indignant sacrificial lamb. It was just so unfair!

Her mind whirled still with the memory of all that had transpired the morning after her debut ball, the events as fresh as a bruise. Gabrielle had arisen that morning with Lord Gregory and their interaction on the veranda was still fresh in her mind. Gabrielle could not shake her anxiety at Lord Gregory's parting words that he would call on her the next day. To Gabrielle, it felt as if an anvil hung above her head, the promise of a mysterious visit hanging like a threatening pall over her. What could he mean?

As much as she longed to postpone rising from the comfort of her bed, at last Gabrielle pushed aside her coverlet and called for her maid. She decided her conservative navy gown would grant her the proper armor to handle any conversation with Lord Stalward should he follow through on his promise to call. She met her parents in the sunroom where they enjoyed breakfast.

"Gabrielle," her mother said once Gabrielle was herself seated with a cup of tea before her, "I must say, your debut was a tremendous success. I received missives from four prospective suitors before dawn, all asking to speak with your father."

Jacques raised the notes and waved them with a chuckle. "Elizabeth, you outdid yourself. I certainly was the proudest husband and father to present their daughter into society."

Jacques leaned in and exchanged a brief kiss with his wife. Gabrielle smiled at them both, reaching for a scone and honey. "Father, you are wonderful for saying so. I must admit it was not as painful an evening as I thought it might be until the ever-so-lovely Lady Deville accosted me," Gabrielle drawled as she bit into the scone.

Elizabeth turned to her daughter with a twinkle in her eye. "Now Gabrielle, you know Lady Deville only means well when imposing her... strong opinions...on everything including, yes, prospective suitors for you and Patrice. You must be patient with her. What was her council on this occasion?" Elizabeth raised her teacup to her delicate lips, which did nothing to hide her mirthful smirk.

Gabrielle sighed, shaking her head. "It was preposterous. She suggested that Lord Stalward was interested in securing my hand in marriage and that I would be well served to accept." Gabrielle laughed. "Can you imagine?"

Elizabeth and Jacques both stiffened, sharing a quick glance at one another which Gabrielle did not miss. Elizabeth recovered first, a mischievous smile playing on the corners of her lips. "Well, that explains the excitement that surged through the ballroom when you and Lord Stalward emerged from the veranda last night."

"What?" Jacques sputtered, "What on earth are you talking about, Elizabeth?" Then, turning to Gabrielle, "Please do not tell me that you were seen walking alone out on the veranda with Lord Stalward. Gabrielle, we cannot afford for you to be involved in any sort of scandal, especially not at your coming-out party."

Gabrielle dabbed her mouth with her napkin before responding. "Father, I did not go out onto the veranda with anyone—you should know me better than that. I am not seeking the attentions of any man, least of all Lord Stalward who barely speaks but to annoy or undermine me! No, it was Lord Stalward who followed me out to the veranda where I had gone to clear my mind after Lady Deville's upsetting confrontation."

Elizabeth and Jacques watched Gabrielle closely, searching for something to assuage their concern. Gabrielle sucked a breath in through her teeth and turned bright pink when she realized their train of thought, responding vehemently. "And nothing happened," Elizabeth sighed out loud in her relief. Her father's eyebrow continued to be raised in question. Gabrielle insisted. "I immediately returned to the ballroom. Damn, those gossips!" Gabrielle's fingers knotted themselves in her lap, the few bits of scone she'd had forming an uncomfortable lump in the pit of her belly.

A gentle cough from the doorway stirred the three of them from the topic and they turned to their maid, Sally, clearing her own throat before announcing the presence of the very gentleman in discussion. "Lord Stalward is here to see you, sir. Ma'am."

Though his unannounced visit would normally come as no surprise, today of all days, Gabrielle felt the flush of hot color creep upon her cheeks at the thought he may have overheard some of their discussion while waiting his announcement.

"Gregory, do come in, come in." Jacques Martin called, standing as Lord Gregory Stalward breezed past Sally and bowed first to Jacques, then more deeply to Elizabeth, who likewise stood. Finally, he bowed to Gabrielle in a low formal bow, even though she remained in her seat, arms crossed under her full bosom and refusing to look at the aforementioned source of her dismay.

Jacques swept his hair with his hand. "You can enlighten us on a subject that we were just discussing. Just why on earth would you address Gabrielle alone and out on the veranda last night in plain sight of all in attendance, for London's gossips to make hay of?"

Gregory took a sharp breath in, his gaze darting almost imperceptibly to Gabrielle, and responded, "Sir Martin... Jacques, all will be explained in due course. I promise you that Gabrielle's reputation was not, and will never be impugned by anyone, ever. Least of all by my actions."

With that, Jacques visibly relaxed, taking back his seat at the table, and offering the lone open chair to Lord Gregory. Gregory declined Jacques offer to sit, continuing, "Sir Martin, I am fine standing, but I would like to ask for a private word with Gabrielle if I may."

Jacques and Elizabeth faced Lord Gregory with narrow eyes. "Lord Gregory, there can be no conversation you wish to have with my daughter that cannot be had in front of her mother and father."

At this Gabrielle stood, as she held her head high, shoulders back, her visage carrying transparent disdain. She would not comply with his request for a private audience with the duke.

Lord Gregory sighed as he walked over to the fireplace. He rested a bronzed hand on the mantlepiece, his head bent low in thought. Gabrielle sucked in her breath feeling a contraction at her throat at what words might tumble out of his mouth. "Very well," he spoke at last, turning to face Gabrielle directly, "I may as well not mince words here. Gabrielle, I am here today to offer for your hand in marriage."

Gabrielle's mouth dropped open, her hand flying to her heart. *What is this?,* she thought, her mind racing. *He has never exchanged one word of pleasantry besides the basic necessities in all these years, and yet here he is asking for my hand in marriage?* Gabrielle shut her mouth and turned quickly around to face her equally stunned parents.

Elizabeth recovered first, though her eyes, too, were wide and shocked. "Lord Gregory, you have certainly taken us all quite by surprise—but, please, do sit down."

Elizabeth laid a gentle but firm hand on her husband's arm, urging Jacques to sit. Lord Gregory sighed deeply, crossing to Elizabeth first as he reached for her chair so she might sit, after which he took his chair at the table. They all turned to look at Gabrielle, urging her to join. Reluctantly, and in a decidedly unladylike manner, Gabrielle finally sat at the furthest end of the table away from Lord Gregory.

"Lord Gregory, you have always been like a son to me and Elizabeth," Jacques said. His voice was measured, deliberate. "But it would not be unreasonable for me to state that my wife and I are more than aware of a certain—distance—between you and my daughter. Marriage into your family, your title, would certainly be advantageous, but we must question … why? And why with so much evident subterfuge?"

Lord Gregory's face remained unreadable for a moment and Gabrielle found herself leaning closer, curious if not eager to hear the man's reasons. If she were honest, she would be forced to shamefully acknowledge that the ghost of his touch on her face last night on the veranda reemerged with an unfamiliar emotion of…longing. She had been mesmerized by the way his eyes had glimmered in the candlelight. As if sensing her thoughts, Lord Gregory shifted his gaze to hers, his worried forehead smoothing out, though a hint of sadness chased across his features. Gabrielle thought with uncharacteristic despondency that this was not the look of a man in love.

Lord Gregory took a deep breath, walking back to grip the fireplace mantle as if for support, with his large hand. "For you all to truly understand how I have arrived here today with this request, there are certainly some things of an unpleasant nature that I must communicate with you." Gregory turned pointedly to Jacques "Jacques, are you certain that I should continue with the ladies present?

"Gregory you know that there are no secrets in this family. Now please get to the point."

FROM WHENCE IT CAME

"*Y*ou'll remember, I'm sure, Jacques," Lord Gregory began, "that auspicious day almost four years ago at White's Club that the esteemed Joseph Bazalgette received word that Parliament would fund the creation of the waterworks system?"

Jacques nodded impatiently. Elizabeth beamed at her husband.

"Of course. Bazalgette is one of my dearest friends and mentors. Without him the waterworks project would never have come to be," Jacques interjected.

"Indeed," Lord Gregory replied. "I, too, remember that day. How you clapped Bazalgette on the shoulder. I believe your words were 'Your vision will save countless lives and bring London to a new age of science and industry.' And I couldn't have agreed more. The cholera outbreaks in the city were worse than ever that year. If I'm being truthful, it is hard for me to believe that any of us, myself included were brave enough to remain in the city and not just run back to Ramsgate where the sun and ocean would have protected us from the impending disease. But I remained… largely because of you and certainly to help you in any way I could with this prestigious appointment."

Jacques chuckled. "It was indeed an auspicious day. I can admit to having a little too much to drink that night."

"I well remember," Elizabeth said, irritation in her tone, but a smile on her face.

Jacques shook his head to bring him back to the present. "This is well and good, Lord Gregory, but I do not see what it has to do with marriage to our Gabrielle."

"Peace." Lord Gregory held out his hands for patience, "I will reveal all that I can. You did have much to drink that night, Jacques, which is why I sent you home in my carriage. And though I stayed a little later to enjoy the revelries, I was quite clear in my mind when I heard what Lord Norwood had to say.

Gabrielle shuddered, remembering Lord Norwood at her debut ball. The man was nothing short of beefy and seemed in Gabrielle's estimation to exist in a constant state of red-face indignation.

"Norwood was at the club late that night," Lord Gregory said, his voice dropping ominously, "And he bragged considerably about how he presumed to take his place as the lead construction for the new sewers of London."

"Of course, he'd never get the contract," Jacques added, "It was an unanimous decision between Bazalguette and myself, supported by most in the Parliament. Norwood's shoddy business is what caused that bridge failure nearly a decade ago! Caused several deaths, if I'm not mistaken, and quite the scandal for his family estate.

"Indeed," Lord Gregory agreed. "Although he still held quite the opinion of himself, bragging that night about how someone low born—forgive me for saying so, sir—as Jacques Martin could refuse his commission. But you did, and London is better for it, though Norwood has grumbled about it ever since."

Gregory took a deep breath as he pondered the best way to approach this situation. He knew the individuals in this party well. Jacques Martin lived a life committed to his personal code of honor and integrity. He would never willingly allow his daughter to be sacrificed on the matrimonial altar, especially under such circumstances, and yet Jacques would relent and do what he knew was best for Gabrielle. As for Elizabeth, she was a smart and worldly woman. Her greatest wish for Gabrielle was to see her marry well, and to someone whom she respected and might even one day come to love.

Gregory continued. "A few weeks ago I brought you news immediately of what I had overheard Norwood discussing at White's." Gregory paused and looked upon Gabrielle, watching as comprehension lifted her brow. " Norwood has continued to make awful accusations against both you and Bazelgette, claims which are not only distasteful but could ruin you both as well as the project we have all invested so much of our lives to launch and ensure in its success."

Gregory watched Gabrielle wince at this, while enlightenment slowly dawned on her beautiful face about the real reason for his surprising marriage proposal. Gabrielle now would understand that this was not a matter of love for Gregory.

He had to admit that under different circumstances, it was true that Gregory would not likely have sought Gabrielle as a proper bride, given her rash, impulsive nature. And, he thought, her brashness was one aspect of Gabrielle's character where Gregory did find fault with Jacques and Elizabeth. But, at the same time, he found Gabrielle wholly becoming, challenging, and intriguing. Even now as Gregory summoned the courage to say what must be said, he could not help but let his eyes fall on Gabrielle, a hot tension coiling in him as he watched the rise and fall of her chest just above the delicate neckline of her gown.

He mentally shook his head, clearing his thoughts and returning to the present. "Jacques," he began again, "I would never desire to be disloyal to you, or anyone in your family. And while I know my proposal must shock you, the truth of the matter is that I find Gabrielle a wholly suitable match for me. I seek only what is best for your family, and mine, and I trust that if we are to be wed, I shall be able to properly guide your daughter in the ways of being an acceptable duchess."

Gabrielle gave a small gasp of surprise, though Gregory could not fathom her shock. He noted, too, that the lines around Elizabeth's delicate mouth tightened a little bit. *This is not going the way I expected at all*, Lord Gregory mused continuing "Jacques, my loyalty to you should never be questioned. You know this. A situation," his eyes flicked to Gabrielle whose cheeks were rosy with indignation, "has arisen that requires a strong response and one that will protect all of you. You are my family, Jaques, Elizabeth. Marrying Gabrielle is a matter of honor for me and all of us. I will not, I cannot shirk this duty."

"What do you mean man? What's this about shirking your duty?" Jacques demanded.

"You know what Norwood has been up to." Gregory paused, unsure if Jacques would want him to continue with the women present.

"Speak up Gregory, I have no secrets from Elizabeth, and frankly Gabrielle has a right to hear this as well," Jacques spoke firmly.

Elizabeth exclaimed, "What claims can that onerous man make against Jacques?"

"Norwood is claiming that Jacques had intentionally brought the cholera to London in the spring of 1849. He claims Jacques hired and brought over prostitutes from the Middle East who were infected with cholera so that he could spread the plague in London and thereby win his cause with Parliament for London's new water and sewage system."

Jacques stood, pressing his hands on the table. "Anyone with any sense knows that this is a lie. Truly, how could anyone believe this? This is the blustering of a jealous man seeking vengeance." Elizabeth reached for her husband's arm, squeezing it reassuringly. Gabrielle stood, still shocked by this terrible accusation.

Gregory looked up at Jacques with sympathetic eyes. "My first reaction was exactly yours. As I said, it was at White's that I first learned of this ridiculous slander. I, too, was incredulous at the audacity of such a lie and protested strongly which quickly turned the tables on Norwood. But it was then that Earl Sinclair, Norwood's father-in-law, proclaimed to the members that this falsehood was the truth. He claims that there was an actual witness who had transported the women to London at your behest. Sinclair told the group that the man had been paid a small fortune to keep this tale to himself, and on his deathbed finally was compelled to expose the truth."

"Jacques," Gregory continued, "as ridiculous as this accusation is to one and all, it is beginning to be accepted as a dead man's confession by some within London. It makes no matter that the messengers were the Norwoods. The members all listened to the Earl Sinclair. He is nobility and not only that, he is powerful and hateful, not unlike his son-in-law. And because so many died during the cholera epidemic it still engenders anger and fear in men's hearts.

"I have thought on how we best can handle this situation but without the power of the Montrose and Stalward houses fully behind you, Jacques, this scandal will not easily be blotted. I have heard that Norwood even approached the London Police—he will not let this alone."

Jacques' brow furrowed in worry and then remembered the immediate issue at hand. "Well, this is some news, but what does it have to do with you and Gabrielle?"

"If Gabrielle marries me, you all will have the full protection of my house. My family name is powerful, more so than Norwood or the Earl of Sinclair. No one will dare contradict or refute our claims of innocence. No one will try and dishonor or impugn you or your family ever again. Norwood will finally be neutralized as a threat, with any hope, permanently. Marriage with Gabrielle will send a message of solidarity to all of London and will unite our causes in more than just words. Dispelling such rumors means your livelihood, and your reputation, remains untarnished."

Across the room, Gabrielle listened to Lord Gregory's revelation in stunned silence. She had long heard the tales of Norwood and his hate for her father. After he'd been awarded the waterworks project, Jacques had insisted on procuring other, more talented contractors, naively as it turned out to be, since he had disregarded the potential consequences of making an enemy of Norwood in the process.

Jacques finally spoke, breaking into his daughter's

musings. "Gregory, I thank you for your offer, and know that it comes from the best place of honor and protection for me and my family name, but I cannot allow you and Gabrielle to become pawns in this disagreement with Norwood. There is nothing he can do to me that I will not be able to survive."

Jacques stood and placed a hand on Lord Gregory's shoulder, which, Gabrielle noticed, had recoiled at her father's pronouncement. "I thank you, my friend," Jacques said again, "but must decline your generous offer."

He then turned to his daughter "Gabrielle you can breathe again. All is well settled."

Gregory shifted in his chair uncomfortable "Jacques, I am sorry but my marriage to Gabrielle is the only possible solution, and there are no longer any other choices."

Jacques' confusion and frustration grew. "Gregory, you are now beginning to try my patience with this talk of conspiracy and absolutes. I am an esteemed member of the Scientific Society of London, and I am one of the engineers for the Crown's greatest modern day engineering venture that has ever been tried. I am not fearful of Norwood and his henchmen. The truth will always be on my side, not his."

Gregory listened, aware of how delicate and sensitive this was going to be, but Gregory had to let Jacques know just how far and duplicitous Lord Norwood would be to sabotage all that Jacques had accomplished.

"Jacques, you are right about everything that you have

said but you cannot combat this attack with the truth alone. We need to fight back and in a united front." Gregory then cleared his throat before he continued, this time readying to fully declare himself to the Martin family.

"Jacques, two things have happened that have made me realize that what I thought was only a perceived threat is real and that the stakes our enemies play at are higher than we could have imagined. This news that the London Police are planning on launching a full investigation, backed by Earl Sinclair himself is entirely true. The damage will not be wound back easily. And the second thing will be impossible to overcome." Gregory looked deeply into his friend's eyes. "And that is ... I have fully compromised Gabrielle's reputation when I met alone with her on the veranda last night at her coming out ball. This, I believe, Norwood will use against your family, a way of casting doubt on the integrity, not only of you but of your whole family. Of course, I immediately took matters into my own hands and professed my love and intention to marry Gabriele to all at White's. The matter has been settled within London, Jacques. Any retraction from me or Gabrielle will mean scandal to your family."

At this, Gregory looked at Gabrielle, whose mouth hung open, eyebrows pulled tightly together in barely contained rage. Gregory sighed and continued, "I never meant—You must believe me that I never meant to place such a shadow across your honor, any of you. But knowing Norwood, I know that he will use this—will use your daughter—as a way to undermine your name, and by extension, the project you have worked so hard to perfect. Though petty, Norwood and Earl Sinclair are powerful and will not stop until they see you stripped of your wealth and status. And while these things alone I know matter not to someone of your character and honor, your diminishment and elimination from history in the role you played to launch London's modernization will be something that you shall grieve the rest of your life. And the scandal to your only child will not be something you will ever be able to survive with any semblance of honor or happiness.

"I promise you, I will honor and protect Gabrielle. We share the love of this family and the desire for its continuance as the basis for our marriage. Most marriages have far less of a foundation." At this Gregory searched Gabriele's face for her thoughts.

Elizabeth quickly interjected. "What of love Gregory? Will Gabrielle be loved by you?"

Gabrielle winced in disgust and frustration, turning her back on all of them embarrassed and humiliated that she should stand in the same room with them all, yet sidelined by each of them.

Gregory found himself blushing slightly as he softly stated, "Elizabeth, not everyone has the benefit of a love match like you and Jacques, but I will do my duty where Gabrielle is concerned and provide her with all she will ever want and need. We will raise fine children together." They all heard but ignored Gabrielle's breath suck into her chest. Gabrielle's cheeks flushed as she found herself staring at him, her gaze defiant though her pulse raced. He calmly turned back to face Elizabeth and stated, "I am sure we will do well together. I certainly do not find this match distasteful."

Gabrielle wanted to scream. She wanted to run at Lord Gregory, beat her fists against his chest, and demand of him that he retract his words. Her hands clenched to fists, the fabric of her satin gloves straining over her tight knuckles. She was so furious that she nearly lost her voice. Nearly … and then her parents sat calmly, so calmly, and Lord Gregory smiled a stupid, satisfied smile. And she found her voice.

"How—dare—you, Gregory?" Gabrielle spat. Three sets of eyes swiveled to hers. "How dare *all* of you! I have sat here this entire time, waiting for someone to speak on my behalf, to defend me and my choices. Well, I see that's not likely to happen so I will speak for myself and what is best for me. Lord Gregory, though I'm sure you find it a *high honor"* Gabrielle's voice dripped with sarcasm. "I cannot marry a man who insists that he will 'do well' with me as if I am some game piece you can fit into your perfect puzzle. You say you find me 'suitable' as if I am some pattern you can match with your drawing rooms! Well, how gallant of you!"

Elizabeth tried to hush her daughter. "Gabrielle please—"

"No, Mother!" Gabrielle rounded on Elizabeth, "He has

been impossibly rude and forward and now it is my turn." She turned toward her tormentor. "Make no mistake, that should I be coerced into this union, for indeed it is *coercion,* I will garner no more satisfaction than you seem to at offering this proposal in the first place. I must thank you, in fact, for confirming for me that marriage in any form is a most distasteful prospect for all women. But that you have forced my hand, holding the threat of family ruin over my head, I cannot see a way to dismiss you outright. You have backed me into a corner, Lord Gregory, one that I shall forever resent being placed in. It is not gentlemanly, sir. Not in the slightest!"

She turned on her heel, facing her parents.

"Father. Mother. Please show me the respect and dignity to allow *me* time to think about this—" Gabrielle paused so she might emphasize her distaste, "You must please allow me the courtesy to make this decision regarding my future on my own. Please do not answer *for* me and do not accept or reject this offer on my behalf."

Gabrielle then walked over to Gregory, straightening her back and raising her chin to him in what she hoped showed haughty defiance. "Lord Stalward, can I trust that on your *gentleman's honor,* you will accept my decision, and my decision alone in this matter? I refuse to be forced into a match, no matter how advantageous you suggest it may be. This is not going to be decided by anyone but me. Will you agree to this, Gregory?"

She extended her hand to Gregory as her stormy blue

eyes pierced his own. Gregory took her hand in both of his. The firmness of his grip, the way his strong hands fully encircled hers, sent a surprising current of fire through Gabrielle. She was horrified to feel her color rising, though not from rage, as their gaze held.

For three days thereafter, Lord Gregory had come by to inquire after Gabrielle, and each time was refused an audience by the loyal and hearty Sally. Gabrielle was unwilling to see Lord Gregory for fear of being rushed or coerced into accepting his proposal, despite how much her mother prevailed upon her to at least pay respects when he visited. As for her Papa, Jacques Martin was so distraught over the entire matter that he could not ask for Gabrielle's cooperation and consideration in good conscience, and so removed himself to his study, informing his wife and staff he was not to be disturbed under any circumstances.

At the end of a rather torturous three days for all the participants, it was decided by the Martin family that they would return to Ramsgate for a few days. Away from Lord Gregory and the bustle and gossip of London, Gabrielle hoped she would be able to think clearly about their next steps. There, at least she had the peace of the countryside and none of the gossips of London haunting their every move. Gabrielle insisted that Jacques leave no word to anyone so that Lord Gregory would not immediately try and follow.

However, the fourth morning after Lord Gregory's proposal, the man had finally had enough, and having gone to the Martin's London home prepared to demand a response from Gabrielle only to discover that the entire family had removed themselves to Ramsgate for several days nearly sent him into outrage. The House of Stalward was the most esteemed and prestigious family line of London society, and although Gregory and his dear deceased father had never relied on their status within society, it was quite another thing for the Martins, friends or not, to so reluctantly embrace what Gregory knew was a noble and generous proposal.

With all haste, Gregory made his way back to his townhome and had his groomsmen prepare his fastest steed. Before the week's end, he would demand Gabrielle's answer.

DECISION AND DESTINY

*R*amsgate was close. Lord Gregory intended to make it to Ramsgate well before nightfall and settle all matters. This game that Gabrielle played by refusing to see him frustrated the duke more than he would have cared to admit. And Jacques, always so sound of mind, was now just as equally infuriating, refusing to see him as well. *Like father, like daughter* was an adage that certainly seemed to be the case in this family. The only Martin with any sense was Elizabeth who, despite their London maid's insistence, still spoke with Gregory each day as he came to visit, encouraging him to be patient with both father and daughter as they found their way through all of the information he'd presented them.

It perplexed him that Gabrielle would not willingly and happily accept his hand in marriage. He knew that her feelings for him were—tolerant—at best, but surely the thought of her own family's well-being ought to outweigh it. He couldn't help but feel his pride sting at the thought that so beautiful a woman—stubborn and infuriating, though she was—might not see her way through to his charms. That he kept thinking of the night on the veranda at Gabrielle's coming out ball was only an added distraction, an irritating one at that. But he found himself often, in the moments before sleep, thinking of the way her skin felt beneath his fingers, the way her lips parted as he looked at her, the rise and fall of her bosom, and, yes, the way he was certain her breath caught as he touched her. For days, he tried desperately to ignore the hardness that invariably grew between his legs every time he thought of Gabrielle coming undone beneath his experienced fingers, hands, and body.

He'd never felt this strange *want* before; any woman he'd ever remotely desired he'd been able to tumble without any resistance. That Gabrielle was proving a challenge to woo intrigued Gregory in the worst way. Not only did he truly want to save the Martin family, so near and dear to his heart, but, selfishly, the thought of Gabrielle finally succumbing to him was tantalizing.

But could she hate him so much that she would risk her father's name and legacy, along with their family's position and title? Why would she defy him so, and refuse to even meet with him about this matter? He seethed with pent up frustration as he thought about Gabrielle. He knew what he must do. Gregory squeezed his muscular thighs about his stallion, urging the horse to move quickly down the road for Ramsgate, less than half a day's journey away.

At Ramsgate, Gabrielle had just dressed for her afternoon ride. As it was a hot day, she had not brought her riding jacket and instead wore only her white linen shirt with the bow tied tight at the collar so her mother would not complain. She needed to ride long and hard. She barely had a moment with her groomsman who tried to convince Gabrielle, unsuccessfully, to place the saddle on her favorite horse, Sebastian. Gabrielle dismissed the groomsman's concerned effort with a kind smile.

Once she rode to the far side of the meadow and into the adjacent forest, Gabrielle continued at a slower pace riding Sebastian onward, her hair loosed from its proper knot by the wind flowing down her back. The air was warmer than she'd expected, and she reached for the bow holding her neckline closed. She wrenched it free and enjoyed the delicious feel of the air kissing her collarbone.

At last, they reached their destination. The small watering hole was Gabrielle's dearest place to visit when she needed time to think or escape. Nestled in a lush clearing, and ringed on all sides by stately trees, the water glistened with the small white cherry blossoms now gently dancing on its surface.

The sun shone through the foliage, making the water

seem to shimmer and dance. Gabrielle slid off Sebastian, guiding him to the edge of the embankment so they could both drink their fill. Sebastian rested, chomping on the grass abutting the pool. Satisfied at last, Gabrielle laid down on her back, letting her linen tunic drape open in a deep V, and shaded her eyes from the sun.

Regrettably, despite the serenity of the spot, Gabrielle's thoughts eventually turned back to the infuriating Lord Gregory. How could this be happening? Surely her father had enough protectors in positions of power, including Stalward himself, to combat any lies and scandal created by a petty and vengeful man like Norwood. Lord Gregory was overreacting. Her father was the most honorable man Gabrielle knew! There could be no man who could ever credibly call into question the character of the man. And yet, the Earl was a petty small man and one in a position of great power.

The timing of this scandal, she knew, could hurt the entire project that her father had committed so great a portion of his life's work. And should Norwood and Sinclair succeed in their duplicitous efforts, and somehow manage to ruin her father's work, Gabrielle would never be able to forgive herself!

Gabrielle sat up onto her elbows, as she tilted her head back in deep thought. She was so engrossed in her thoughts, so deeply satisfied by the warmth of the sun on her face, that she did not notice the soft, slow plod of another horse's hooves through the underbrush. Lord

Gregory had been riding all day and immediately upon arriving at the Martin's home in Ramsgate, went in search of the whereabouts of his reckless prospective wife. Her groomsman informed Gregory of Gabrielle's state of mind as she had ridden off. Gregory's sixth sense brought him to the one place that he knew that Gabrielle always escaped to since she was a wee child just barely able to mount her horse. Gregory weaved his way into the woodland and spotted the thick patch of foliage, in between which he knew would be a pool. He urged his stallion forward quietly and finally reached the edge of the trees. The clearing stretched before him, a true hidden paradise.

There, at the embankment was Gabrielle's white steed, Sebastian. And just beyond him, lay Gabrielle. Her head hung back, golden hair trailing in the grass, and from his vantage point, Gregory could see the curve of her graceful neck arching down her collarbone and then, to his shock, her loosened shirt, low enough at the neck that the barest breeze lifted the fabric, exposing the soft curve of her breasts.

Gregory's breathing hitched and he swallowed hard. Beneath the thin fabric of her shirt, he could see the peaks of her taut nipples shadowed beneath the cloth. He knew he had to shake himself from his reverie, knew he had to compose himself before stepping towards her. The strain of his erection pushed at the fabric of his trousers.

She truly was perfection. Gregory was dumbfounded watching her, wondering how he could have remained oblivious to her all these years as she grew into this beauty, surprised by the errant thought that found him pleased that she might soon be his wife. Several deep breaths, and he'd pulled himself together. Schooling his face into one of nonchalance, he slid off his horse and stepped into the clearing.

"Gabrielle, I see you are fit for a chat." Lord Gregory's voice jolted Gabrielle from her reverie. She scrambled to her feet, brushing blades of grass from her hair. Lord Gregory raised his eyebrow at seeing her dressed like a stable boy, albeit a beautiful one.

"Certainly, as fit as you are sir." Gabrielle pointedly perused Gregory's dusty riding coat and muddied boots before she continued in a haughty tone. "But as you can see, I was perfectly content with my solitude, so please do excuse me." She turned away from him under the pretense of seeing to Sebastian.

"Not so fast Gabrielle," Gregory responded in a low, tight voice. "You cannot keep putting me off, especially as all of London is speaking about our impending marriage. Do you think to make a fool of me? Even as I seek to help you and your family?"

"Lord Stalward, I am not interested in making a fool of you, so if you believe that is the case, do not seek to find the fault with me, but in yourself. Further, if it vexes you so, please feel free to withdraw your proposal." Gabrielle stood her ground, despite longing to seek escape.

"You have always been rash, Gabrielle, but I hardly

thought you to be so dismissive of your family name." Gregory kneeled at the embankment to drink, and splash water on his face.

"Lord Stalward, you are not my husband, and may never be, thus you have absolutely no say in any of my decisions." Gabrielle bit her lip. She knew that she should avoid an argument since tempers were high, and yet she felt so very cornered, both by Lord Gregory's proximity and his proposal.

"Gabrielle," Lord Gregory began, albeit with a softer tone, "I realize this is not anything you expected or sought. You are very young and still immature." Gabrielle's eyes flicked brightly with rage as he continued. "I am sure you hoped for—well, someone who would defer to you and play the besotted lover. I cannot offer you a fairytale love as the other suitors at your debut might have, and I won't pretend to. But I am offering you honor, safety for you and your family, and my undying loyalty."

Gabrielle scoffed. "Lord Stalward, despite our years together you know nothing of me. I despise the idea of marriage, and I am not one to fall in love with any sop. In this, I can assure you that you have erred." She paused, taking a step toward him. "No sir, my frustration is that I feel trapped. Trapped by a society where women have no voice and no control over their very own lives. I feel trapped by the presumption that not only *should* I marry, but that I should *want* to at all. But most of all, I feel trapped by arrogant men like you who assume you can swoop in, save the day, and claim me as some kind of reward in the process!"

Her hands clenched and unclenched into fists at her side and a fiery flush rose to her cheeks. Her bosom heaved with every breath and so furious was she that she hardly noticed the neckline of her linen shirt pulling lower and lower across her breastbone. Gregory could not help but let his eyes drop to the smooth skin there, how it flushed with the woman's anger and heaved with every passionate breath. Gabrielle noticed his eyes blaze, the slight flare of his nostrils, but mistook it for responding irritation.

"Gabrielle," Gregory said, wrenching his eyes away from her breasts, "Try and consider that this may be a true match of our minds. You are unique. You seek your independence. Well, perhaps in this marriage of practicality, we can negotiate terms that satisfy us both. I have wealth and a title that will forgive you any societal improprieties. You can live as a free woman. In turn, I will finally be officially off the marriage market. With you as my Duchess, I can now be truly free of my matrimonial duties. Of course, we will have children, but perhaps, in time, we can also live as friends in every other way."

Gabrielle's mind reeled. Friends? A child? Her hands flew to her cheeks as she turned to face the water. This was insanity…or was it? Gabrielle paused, trying to calm her riotous thoughts. "Lord Gregory," she finally called over her shoulder, "I know that I truly may have no other choice to preserve my family name and, more importantly, my father's work, but I beg of you to let me think on this a bit more. I need time—until tomorrow. Give me until then."

She turned to face him, only to find that he'd advanced on her while her back was turned. He stood no more than an arm's breadth away, the intensity in his gaze stealing the breath from her. Gabrielle looked up into his eyes which seemed to burn with fire. She realized in that moment that her shirt was still open at her chest, revealing the top of the soft mounds of her breasts. She realized this at the same time that she made no move to cover herself, meeting Lord Gregory's fiery gaze with a defiant one of her own. Their locked stares sent a shiver racing through her, hardening her nipples against the cool breeze and the light friction of her shirt.

"I know I am not your choice," Lord Gregory murmured, close enough that his breath stirred little hairs on Gabrielle's forehead, "I know you do not love me, Gabrielle. But I do see other ways we might be— advantageous—to one another. I hope you will give me the chance to show you one day."

"Other ways, Lord Gregory?" Gabrielle's breath hitched. His eyes, oh God, his eyes were so intense, so deep Gabrielle thought she might fall into them forever. What right had he to possess such spell-binding eyes?

Then, as if in slow motion, Lord Gregory's eyes dropped again to her breasts where Gabrielle felt a single drop of sweat slide over her collarbone and down, down, between her breasts. The entire world froze for a moment.

And then, in one swift movement, Lord Gregory dragged her body against his, strong hands gripping her arms firmly, though not painfully. Lord Gregory's eyes were an inferno and Gabrielle felt herself melting. Electricity gripped them both. They were close enough that their noses brushed one another, yet Gabrielle made no move to push him away.

"Gregory, what are you doing?" Gabrielle whispered against his lips, her deep blue eyes seeking an answer within the depths of his.

Gregory whispered, "Showing you an advantage."

With that, his lips crashed into hers. His mouth was warm, she realized, and soft. At first, she knew not what to do but after a moment, she relaxed into the feel of his lips pressed to hers and slowly parted her lips in return, a soft sigh escaping. Gregory's answering groan lit a fire within her as they deepened their kiss. Gregory sucked her lower lip between his teeth, nipping gently before shifting so his tongue could seek out her own.

Gabrielle broke away just long enough to wrap her arms around Gregory's neck before their mouths met again. Gregory's hands dove into long hair, gathering fistfuls of it, as she instinctively raked her hands along his broad shoulders. Gregory groaned deeply as he released one hand from her hair, down her back, and gripped her buttocks, hauling her against him even harder. Gabrielle was shocked to feel the press of him through his trousers, a hard length that felt—oh God, he felt huge—and she was even more surprised to feel an answering slickness in her own trousers, a heat that coiled low and delicious in her abdomen.

She gasped against his lips, tilting her head back as he trailed kisses down her neck and ear with abandon that made the hard press of his erection twitch against her belly. Her hardened nipples rubbed his chest through her shirt and she arced into the friction. Gabrielle was compelled by some force deep inside her to yield, gasping, as Gregory forced her backwards taking slow steps until her back met a tree. Their bodies leaned into each other, Gregory's knee pressing between her legs and rubbing—oh God, she needed that feeling—so perfectly at the apex of her thighs that Gabrielle found herself rocking back and forth against the curve of his thigh. She was powered by an inexplicable force, with no idea what end was to come, only that she needed more of this, of him, pressing against all planes of her body, making that friction coil tighter and tighter between her legs.

Gabrielle felt a frenzied heat forming in her low abdomen and for one reckless moment, she thought of plunging her own hands into her trousers to ease the ache, the wetness she felt pooling there. She could not control her thoughts or her throbbing body. She needed more. She grasped at Gregory's topcoat and tried to move her hands beneath his shirt so she could touch his chest. She needed skin, the feeling of his skin on hers. She was a woman desperate, clutching at him as his mouth returned to hers, swallowing her panting with a deep kiss. He growled as she continued to move her hands down his chest, frantically searching for an opening in his jacket.

Gabrielle smiled at this and continued her sweet torture, until Gregory finally grasped her wrists in one of his hands, pulling them over her head and pinning them to the tree trunk. Here he paused to stare down at her swollen lips, the way her breaths came in ragged gasps. Gregory smiled and used his free hand to gently sweep the opened collar of her shirt lower, undoing one or two buttons of her shift until her breasts were bared, nipples pink and peaked, resting on the shelf of her stays. With a guttural groan, Gregory dipped his head down until his lips just brushed the tip of her nipple, his free hand cupping her other breast.

Gabrielle whimpered involuntarily, the brush of his lips on her igniting an inferno through her whole body. At her moan, Gregory lost his composure, sucking her nipple into his mouth and making Gabrielle cry out. Oh, she had never felt anything like this—the electricity of it—as his tongue circled and sucked her nipple hungrily, his free hand rubbing and flicking her other nipple with a callused thumb.

"Oh...oh..." Gabrielle gasped as her knees buckled beneath her. Gregory's leg, still propped between both of hers was the only thing keeping her from sinking to the ground in her ecstasy. He moved his mouth to her other breast, sucking harder as she arced to meet his tongue. When she thought, at last, that she might come undone, when the very cusp of a release seemed near enough to touch, Gregory dropped her arms and stepped away, leaving Gabrielle trembling and gripping the tree behind her. Her eyes were luminous, her breasts slick with his kisses, her hair a wild tangle. It was all Gregory could do to take another step back, to quell the explosion he felt too near in his own heated body.

"I think we will do very well together Gabrielle…. very well," he said between his ragged breaths. He then straightened and firmly swept both hands through his hair as he shook his head, and began methodically buttoning his shirt, and topcoat, and finally fixing the bulge in his pants as he walked away.

Gabrielle was not as quickly able to compose herself. She turned facing the water, her body moist everywhere, filled with a longing she could not comprehend. Her lips were swollen from Gregory's kisses. The cool air brushed her erect nipples and made her wince in what felt like pleasure intermingled with pain. She felt somehow uncomfortable, unsatisfied, and yet altogether amazed by their transgression.

Gabrielle suddenly found herself embarrassed by her total submission to Gregory, the way her entire body responded to him, needed him closer. She rearranged her clothing in a daze. Behind her, she was dimly aware of the sounds of Gregory mounting his horse. As he galloped away, she heard him say "You have until tomorrow

Gabrielle". She shivered more so because of their recent lovemaking than his threatening words.

Gabrielle was not completely innocent in the actions of love; her Mama had taken some time when she was much younger to explain the ways of the marriage bed, but always with the notion that, especially at a younger age, it was something to be avoided rather than embraced. She had no idea, though, none at all, that such acts could illicit such joy, such satisfaction. And yet, for all the pleasant buzzing she felt in her body, she still felt unsatisfied, unfulfilled, and empty.

Still in her daze, Gabrielle mounted Sebastian restraining him to a saunter without a backward glance at the glade.

PROMISES MADE

*A*s he had promised, Gregory relented to Gabrielle's request for one more day before giving him her final decision on his marriage proposal. Gabrielle, in turn, spent the remainder of the day locked in her room thinking about nothing else but what had transpired between she and Gregory only a few hours earlier. She could still taste Gregory in her mouth, feel his sinewy arms wrapped about her, the way his hand pinned both of her wrists, holding her in firm but gentle submission, the way he hungrily trailed kisses on her body. Gabrielle tingled from head to toe and was too embarrassed by her thoughts to even consider meeting with her parents or maid. Suddenly the thought of marriage to Gregory brought forth a stirring in her heart and loins that felt like excitement.

Later that evening, the Martin family enjoyed a quiet

dinner at Ramsgate. Gabrielle was noticeably quiet and withdrawn. Any attempt made by Elizabeth or Jacques for conversation elicited only one-word responses from the distracted Gabrielle. Once dinner had finally been cleared by the servants, Gabrielle placed her napkin on the table, and stood with her head held high, as she laid her hands on the table.

"I have made my decision." She looked at both her parents. "I will marry Gregory, Lord Stalward." Gabrielle raised her hand up to stop her father who started to protest. "Father, no. This must be done. And truly, I will make this work with Gregory, for we have no secrets between us, nor do we harbor any unrealistic, ridiculous hope for love. We will be friends as we have always been. Nothing will change."

Gabrielle did not dare look at her mother when she made this declaration of her proposed platonic relationship with the handsome Lord. Gabrielle rounded the table, giving each of them a quick kiss on the cheek before quickly retreating to her room and leaving her parents stunned and speechless at the dinner table.

The next day, Gregory was back in his London townhouse at his father's grand mahogany desk, trying unsuccessfully to focus on estate work and instead being distracted by thoughts of Gabrielle that invaded his mind. He had dreamt about her unfettered passion when they kissed, both in sleep last night and upon waking the following morning. He'd always thought Gabrielle a beauty, but never in his wildest dreams did he imagine she would respond to him so completely. The memory of her soft lips, her full breasts in his hands, was enough to send him into a stupor. But almost as soon as those thoughts entered his brain, they were chased by the practicalities of a union with Gabrielle. She was stubborn, he knew, but it distressed him greatly that she would put him off so long and at the expense of her own family. She may not trust his intentions, or perhaps she did but at any rate, it made her postponement even more infuriating in the wake of what Gregory knew could be on the horizon for the Martin family should Lord Norwood be able to sink his teeth into the rumor mill.

Gregory's head spun at the thought of his would-be-intended's stubborn nature. How could she even think of rejecting him? Gregory felt his blood boil as he ran a hand through his thick hair and leaned back sighing heavily. Gregory knew he should be objective and rational but could not shake his anxiety at the thought of her rejection. He chose to think instead that this niggling worry he was feeling was a matter of his real concern over the Martin's safety and well-being if his plan was not implemented, rather than accept his concern was also an issue of his ego and self-respect, or even worse, lend any serious credence to the idea that his heart was now invested in Gabrielle's decision.

Just then his manservant knocked on the door of his study. "Come in," Gregory replied sitting up in his chair. "Yes, Tobias. What is it?"

"Lord Stalward, you have a message from Ramsgate."

Gregory quickly stood and reached for the notecard. After scanning the contents, a slow smile spread across his face. He reached for a cigar after carefully placing the card into the top drawer of his secretary table and leaned back in his red leather chair. There were only two words simply and neatly written on the notecard.

"I accept."

PLANS SET IN MOTION

"*G*abrielle is this rumor about you and Lord Stalward then true?" Patrice searched her friend's eyes. Patrice, having hurried over at the first news of Gabrielle's betrothal, had learned of the rumor from her maid and then confirmed it with Lord Rittenhouse who had called on her shortly after Gabrielle's debut ball. She'd intended to visit her friend regardless; her parents had of late been inquiring more and more about the handsome, but roguish James Rittenhouse who had called upon Patrice, not once but twice since Gabrielle's debut ball. Though Patrice's parents, the Corchorans, had chosen to follow their own calling, both in profession and marriage, that did not stop them from feeling some concern about the attentions of Lord Rittenhouse. Nonetheless, the Corchorans would keep their minds open regarding the controversial Lord Rittenhouse and judge for themselves if he was a worthy man and potential suitor for their beloved Patrice. Patrice had anxiously sought Gabrielle's opinion on the matter, that is until she discovered Gabrielle's own series of events which were far more compelling now.

"Gabrielle, is it true? Are you to marry Lord Stalward?" Patrice and Gabrielle sat outside on the veranda, the sun shining down on them.

Gabrielle sighed. "Patrice, I think I have no choice." Gabrielle would not disclose to anyone, even her dear Patrice, the true reason for her hasty marriage, the threats from Lord Norwood and the potential harm to her father's legacy. Gabrielle had long decided that to put her friend in particular in the middle of it all would be horrendous since Lord Norwood was, in fact, Patrice's uncle through marriage to her Aunt Clara, her mother's sister.

"Why? Why no choice Gabrielle?" Patrice demanded her response. Gabrielle stood and turned her back.

"We were..." Gabrielle paused, searching for a suitable explanation. She decided on something somewhat near the truth. "We were caught in a compromising position. So we have no choice, you see. For our names and reputations, Lord Gregory is forced to do the honorable thing by me."

"So that part of the rumor is also true then?" Patrice's brows furrowed.

"What part of the rumor? Please Patrice what are the gossips saying?" Gabrielle implored her friend.

Patrice went on. "The rumor is that the evening of your debut ball, while you and the duke were out on the veranda, he had his way with you." Gabrielle smiled at that, thinking that the gossip was only helping their cause. "And they are saying that it was only after being threatened by your Papa that the duke would marry you."

Gabrielle winced at this but then quickly recovered. "Well, they are correct in one way, the duke did compromise me and because of this I must now marry him."

"Oh, Gabrielle!" Patrice rose and grasped her friends' hands in hers. "You cannot marry Gregory. You will have other excellent suitors and you will forget this happened soon enough!"

"Patrice, my friend." Gabrielle hugged her tightly and then pulled away. "I have never truly sought to marry, you know. Perhaps in this way, the Duke and I will suit each other very well as he does not particularly wish to marry me, either. He has promised I will be able to live my life as I choose; I will travel, ride, and see you as much as I please." Gabrielle smiled and tilted her head slightly towards Patrice. "Patrice nothing will change! And anyway, love is a fanciful notion for those who can afford to play or have nothing to lose!"

Patrice's mouth drew into a thin line, clearly doubting her friend. Gabrielle ignored Patrice and continued confidently. "No, I will marry for duty and my freedom. One thing I do know is Gregory's character. I can trust the man to not interfere with how I choose to spend my days."

"But Gabrielle, what of your nights? Will you be

comfortable sharing his bed?" Patrice whispered, looking over her shoulder to ensure no one was there. "He will want an heir and as he is a young and virile man, he will want to consummate your marriage in all ways. Have you thought about this?"

Gabrielle's cheeks warmed under Patrice's scrutiny. "I will never look on the duke as a lover, but I do respect him... like a brother." Gabrielle's heartbeat quickened at this lie. She still felt his hot breath on her skin and how it sent a current throughout her body. Gabrielle felt like a besotted schoolgirl. But she could not yet confess out loud her passion for the duke as it was all too new and strange.

"Gabrielle, you are not a pretender." Patrice's voice dropped low. "I don't know that you will ever be able to sustain a lie of this magnitude over time. But I cannot advise you not to pursue the marriage. Your reputation and consequently, your parents' reputation requires that this marriage happen, whether for good or bad. I am so sorry, Gabrielle."

"As am I Patrice. As am I." Gabrielle placed her arm through Patrice's "Now let's return to Mama." The girls walked out of the room, their heads close together hanging like sad dogs as they shut the door behind them.

NEW BEGINNINGS

Mr. and Mrs. Jacques Martin
request the honor of your presence at the wedding of their
daughter
Gabrielle Louisa Martin
&
Duke, Lord Gregory, Edward Charles Stalward IV of
Montrose
Saturday, October 1st, at noon Bellbridge Church
Ramsgate, England.
A reception will immediately follow at the Montrose Estate
in Ramsgate.

_T_he missives were sent, and responses were received. There would be over three hundred Londoners attending the highly anticipated wedding of Miss Gabrielle Martin and Lord Gregory Stalward. Among the attendees, Norwood would certainly be there.

As this was considered an early fall affair, the women would be wearing the silky new linen garments which were all the rage from France and Italy, and Gabrielle had visited the modiste for a wedding gown of similar styling. The week of the wedding, Patrice and Gabrielle spent countless hours fitting their various dresses, as well as Gabrielle's bridal and honeymoon trousseau. It was a tedious affair, one in which Gabrielle often complained and railed against all that women must go through "for only one blasted afternoon," but Patrice helped lighten the mood with her enthusiasm and humor.

Jacques and Elizabeth agreed with Lord Gregory that the reception would take place at the duke's manse in Ramsgate. At Lord Gregory's request, no detail or expense was spared. Knowing that this wedding was already a cause for some speculation, he intended that the event itself would be above reproach.

The morning of the wedding, the sun cast bright beams through the windows of Gabrielle's room, puddling in warm, gleaming spots on the wood floor. The air was light, with just a hint of autumnal crispness, and Gabrielle took a deep breath as Patrice helped spread her veil gently along the long train of her white silk gown. Gabrielle clutched her bouquet of aromatic white and pink roses, orchids, and apple blossoms, all tied in a perfect bow made of a simple velvet ribbon to keep her hands from their inevitable trembling.

At last, she glimpsed herself in the mirror and could not help the small gasp that escaped her. Gabrielle's golden, thick wavy hair was swept up into a loose and intricate braid, apple blossoms and pearls embedded in each glorious plait that draped over her right shoulder. Her blue eyes were accentuated with just a trace of the black liner that had become so in fashion, making her eyes appear even deeper and of a more violet hue. Her moist and luscious lips were further enhanced by just a kiss of beet juice. Her gown clung to every curve, her bodice open just enough to reveal smooth, golden skin and the cleavage of her ample bosom. Elizabeth and Patrice, who looked on at the beautiful bride in the mirror both sighed.

"Yes, you will do." Elizabeth smiled.

Patrice hugged her friend, their eyes meeting in the mirror before them. "Oh, Gabrielle, truly you are the most beautiful bride that ever was."

Elizabeth handed her daughter one last gift: a pair of sapphire and diamond earrings which brought out the sparkling light of her eyes. The earrings were a Montrose family heirloom and were a gift from Lord Gregory.

Gabrielle tried to quell the shaking in her hands and the faint nausea in her gut as she and her attendants made their way to the back of the church at Ramsgate. She'd known Lord Gregory all her life and despised him for most of it, yet perhaps the most terrifying thing of all was how her entire view of the man altered in so short a time. That he could have such an effect on her was frightening and exhilarating all at once, and the thought that all the attendees might see her nerves on full display only added to her trepidation. It was not like Gabrielle to shy away from anything, yet here she was scared to move forward. Her father, looking dashing and debonair, winked as he approached her, arm ready to escort her down the aisle. All eyes turned to look upon the beautiful bride and her dapper father.

Gabrielle's eyes shone as she looked up to the church altar and caught the first sight of Lord Gregory, dressed in all his regal finery, and could not help but blush at the sight of him. Gregory held her gaze and an electric current seemed to sweep between them. Lord Gregory was mesmerized as he watched Gabrielle approach; his only thought was how lucky he was to be marrying a woman he found so…compelling. Never mind her temper and stubborn nature, Gabrielle was unique and interesting, and he found himself looking forward to spending his time and energy taming her disposition. The lessons would begin tonight, in their bedchamber.

Lord Gregory smiled at the thought just as James Rittenhouse, the best man loudly cleared his throat, shaking him back to the present moment as the vicar and Gabrielle's father waited patiently for him to come and accept his bride before the altar.

Standing so close to Gregory, Gabrielle, too, had thoughts of romantic encounters with Lord Gregory, and she fought the urge to lean into his broad chest and kiss him as she had in the clearing, despite her misgivings of entering the marriage. Gabrielle's heart raced and her cheeks flushed at the thought of what more passion would unleash. She smiled, shaking the thoughts from her mind as she accepted his hand to ascend the altar and take their vows.

With the final pronouncement of "man and wife," she heard the guests clapping their hands in congratulations, as she leaned into Gregory's kiss. His lips met hers softly, chaste in comparison to what she remembered from the pond, but it nevertheless shook her to the core. Amused laughter reminded the couple that they were not alone, and Gabrielle pulled away quickly with a quick rush of pink to her cheeks.

The couple enthralled the crowd, engendering whispers of praise and jealousy. As Gabrielle and Gregory exchanged their vows, Patrice Corchoran looked on smiling, oblivious to the admiring stares of eligible bachelors in attendance, though perhaps none more so than the best man, Lord

James Rittenhouse who's smoldering gaze rested upon the beautiful Patrice.

Patrice smiled, looking to Gabrielle who had just answered the clergyman: "Yes, I will take you, Duke, Lord Gregory Edward Charles Stalward IV, to be my husband for richer or poorer, in sickness and in health, until death us do part."

Patrice watched the handsome couple kiss and took in a deep breath just as her eyes met James' seeking gaze. But Patrice refused to dwell on James Rittenhouse and the strained flirtation they shared. Today was a day for celebration and to fortify her dearest friend Gabrielle with strength and love.

The reception that followed was truly an event remembered for the ages. Lord Gregory insisted on sparing no expense to the wedding plans, enlisting Elizabeth's fine eye for detail to arrange flowers, candles, silver, and place settings to perfection. They engaged Her Majesty's finest orchestra and the music swelled as champagne flowed.

Breaking with convention, the bride and groom asked both the best man and maid of honor to toast them. James and Patrice regaled the guests with happy stories of the couple when they were very young and dismissive of one another. Gabrielle and Gregory laughed along, seeming to truly enjoy themselves.

Only one among the guests was not delighted by the events of the day, and indeed remained scowling at his table all evening: Lord Alfred Norwood. His wife, Patrice's Aunt Clara, looked her usual frail self, sitting complacently next to her odious husband. Clara made no effort to engage in pleasantries with him and instead focused her attention on her beautiful niece. Norwood sat and watched the events through his bloodshot lizard eyes. Gabrielle noticed him immediately. It was impossible not to notice a man of that girth. But his eyes were what she most remembered that day. His red eyes seemed to brew with poison. Gabrielle shivered slightly as she returned her gaze up to her husband. *Husband...*she could hardly believe it. Lord Gregory, her impossible Gregory, was now her husband.

So absorbed was Gabrielle, and indeed everyone, in the exuberance of the wedding feast, that no one noticed the Norwood's early departure. Just as Norwood cast a final look back, he watched the crowd swoon in delight when Jacques Martin tapped his smiling son-in-law to request a dance with his daughter, while Lord Gregory Stalward claimed the hand of his mother-in-law.

Gabrielle had to admit, she was having more fun than she anticipated. She smiled up at her father as he danced with her around the ballroom. He looked into her eyes, now bright and luminous with champagne.

"My dear Gabrielle," he said, "You look happy. I pray you are."

Gabrielle replied, "Father, you don't need to worry. I am content, truly."

"But I want more than contentment for you. I wish you to feel a deep love like your mother and I have been so blessed to share."

Gabrielle glanced at Lord Gregory, still dancing with her mother. Elizabeth laughed brightly at something Lord Gregory whispered. Their eyes met just then, and they both smiled. Gabrielle turned back to her Papa, saying softly, "Don't worry Papa. I feel sure that all will be well in the end."

As the evening drew to conclusion, Gabrielle and Gregory met once more at the middle of the dance floor for a final turn.

"The gossips must surely be satisfied," Gabrielle whispered to her husband.

Lord Gregory laughed, a buoyant sound. "As long as you, too, my wife, are also satisfied."

"I'm thinking I may be," Gabrielle quipped back.

At last, the final guests departed. All those staying at the estate with the newlyweds found their respective bedchambers. Gabrielle and Gregory, as was custom, took the largest suite: a palatial space with two bedrooms adjoined by a sitting room each with a private bath. Gabrielle was escorted to her room alone and was overwhelmed as the silence of her bedchamber fell over her. Impatient and desperate to quell her nerves, Gabrielle asked her maid to draw a bath, wondering where her husband could be. Now that the turmoil and buzz of the wedding ended, Gabrielle found herself too alone with her thoughts.

She wondered if he would even come for her tonight. She both longed and dreaded the idea of seeing him in her bedchamber. The candles flickered as a cool breeze from the open window found its way to the bath. When the water turned tepid, Gabrielle finally shivered and stood, retrieving a pink silk duster from a nearby chair. Gabrielle sat on the edge of the bath and grabbed her brush. Before she'd finished combing through all her hair, Gabrielle heard a knock on the door. She stopped brushing mid-stroke, her breath lodged in her throat.

The knock came again. After a pause, Lord Gregory whispered just loud enough for her to hear, "Gabrielle, it's me."

Taking a deep breath against the flutter in her stomach, Gabrielle replied, "Come in."

Gregory found her in the bathroom still perched on the edge of the tub. He was, Gabrielle noted, like a man transfixed and she delighted in the way his eyes widened and he froze mid-step when he beheld her. Her damp hair and wide blue eyes glistened in the candlelight, her duster wet and clinging to her gentle curves.

Lord Gregory cleared his throat as he whispered hoarsely, "You are beautiful Gabrielle. I thought earlier today that I would never see you look more radiant than the moment you walked down the aisle, but I was proven wrong, yet again, madam." He reached gently for her hands and raised her to stand before him.

"Yet again, Milord?" Gabrielle teased. "When have you been wrong about me before, Lord Gregory?" She swept past him into her bedchamber turning her head to look back at him over her shoulder as she clutched the duster to her bosom.

"Please, Gabrielle, I'd think after today you could call me naught but Gregory. I admit I wasn't certain how you would receive me tonight. And I was wrong in thinking you could not be more beautiful than you were this morning. Yet here you are before me, the most breathtakingly beautiful woman I have ever seen."

Gregory grasped Gabrielle's elbows gently. She sighed, recognizing an urgency in his eyes met equally in her own body. Flashes of his mouth on hers, his hands roaming her body under the tree by the pond, entered her mind.

An innocent, Gabrielle was not prepared for the molten feeling in her body. She reached up to Gregory's broad shoulders, smiling as she slid her fingers beneath his silk jacket. He tensed only slightly, perhaps surprised by her boldness, but then relaxed into her touch as she traced his collarbone, his shoulders, and down to his chest. He took a small step back from her, though his gaze never wandered from her own, as he slid his dressing gown off his shoulders and let it drop to the floor.

Gabrielle took in the sight of her husband, bare in front of her, the candlelight in the room gilding every muscle, every angle, of his form. Her breath hitched and the molten feeling in her body quickly pooled between her legs, creating a delicious heat that made her squirm.

Gregory was a full head taller than her, and all sinewy muscle that hinted at long days spent working in the sun. His sculpted chest was dusted with fine brown hairs. His waist and hips were slim, his legs long and sculpted. When her eyes trailed down his body, taking in the sight of his full, erect manhood, she nearly swooned. Gabrielle knew the way of sexual relations after her work spent in the stables, and indeed, her mother had also spoken to her in hushed tones of the 'marital duty' that would be expected of her. Though nothing could have prepared her for the way her body responded to her husband's gleaming manhood; she only just managed to refrain from sinking to her knees before him, desperate to kiss every hard, smooth inch of him. Her eyes wandered back up to his dark gaze.

He stepped to her again, pressing his erection to her belly, and Gabrielle's lips parted at the heat of it. She wondered briefly how he was to fit inside her, but dismissed the thought as her robe brushed against his bare shaft, making Gregory gasp. Gabrielle knew then that his need was as great as hers. Impulsively, she stood on her tiptoes and brushed his hair with her fingers. At this simple act of intimacy, Gregory groaned deeply grasping her buttocks in his hands as he raised her just enough so that she could feel the hard length of him slip between her own legs, rubbing against her inner thigh.

It was like a fire suddenly swept them both away. Gregory lifted her off the ground as she wrapped her legs around his waist. He carried her to the poster bed where he lay Gabrielle down on her back with such tenderness her heart ached. It was then that her duster fell open, the cool evening breeze racing goosebumps across her skin and hardening her nipples. She couldn't help the tremble that worked its way through her body; she knew she trusted Gregory, but the fear of the unknown still shook her. Sensing her trepidation, Gregory brushed a lock of hair away from her eyes and cradled her chin in his hand.

"Gabrielle," he whispered, "Gabrielle, look at me."

Gabrielle met his gaze with her own dazed eyes, her lips parted and wet.

"I would never hurt you," Gregory murmured. He traced her jaw with his thumb, exactly the way he had that night on the veranda, achingly gentle, and suddenly any nerves Gabrielle had about what lay ahead for them was now replaced with a deep longing.

"I know," she said. Gabrielle reached up to her husband, tracing the line of his collarbone again and relishing that she could see the goosebumps rise along his arms. That she might have such control over his body with the most feather-light touch brought a smile to her lips. Gregory dropped his hand from her jaw to trace the line from the hollow of her collarbone down to her navel, stopping to draw a lazy circle first around her right breast, then her left.

The slow, gentle torture made Gabrielle wriggle

beneath him as she finally snapped, grabbing his shoulders and drawing Gregory to her, thrusting her hips up so that his hot erection rubbed once more between her thighs.

"Gabrielle, patience, or this will be over before it's begun," Gregory said, his voice low and husky. He bent towards her and claimed her in a deep kiss, parting her lips so their tongues could meet. When they broke apart, both were breathless. Gabrielle grunted gently and bit his shoulder as he laced his fingers in hers, pinning her hands on either side of her face. Gregory rocked between her thighs, running the smooth heat of his manhood along her soft skin. Gabrielle whimpered and writhed beneath him, her fears of before long forgotten amid this need coiling deep in her belly. She thrust her hips desperately, unknowingly seeking the satisfaction she longed for.

Gregory nipped her neck and ears and slowly began his descent, first to her cleavage, showering her two perfect breasts with gentle kisses. Each was sweet torture for Gabrielle. When, at last, his mouth clamped firmly over one nipple, Gabrielle whimpered, a shudder wracking her body. A slick wetness seeped from between her legs, a wetness which Gregory sensed as the desperate slide of his erection against her thigh began a more feverish pace. He sucked her nipple harder then, flicking the tip with his teasing tongue.

Her hands were still pinned by his, but Gabrielle was growing increasingly desperate to hold him close to her, to grip his shoulders and let her nails dig into his skin. A need burned deep inside her, and she wanted, demanded, satisfaction for this burn, though she was unsure how. Finally, Gregory released her nipples from his devastating kisses as he resumed his methodical descent down her abdomen, licking her belly button and then kissing and nibbling lightly below to her hip bones. At last, he'd traveled far enough down her body that he released her hands, which she immediately thrust into his hair. Her body glistened with sweat and, at last, she felt his breath against the inside of her legs, the very place where moments before his massive phallus teased her.

Gregory groaned softly, placing kiss after kiss along her inner thighs and Gabrielle heard her voice begging, "Gregory … please, please, please."

She was wet, so wet already, pulsing and aching with this new need he evoked in her. Gregory laughed, low and guttural, as he finally looped her legs one over each of his shoulders, pinning her hips down with his strong, broad hands.

Unlike his first kisses, the sweep of Gregory's tongue between her gleaming, wet folds was claiming and deep. Gabrielle cried out, grasping his hair, and opening her legs as wide as she could. Gregory moaned as his tongue worked, flicking long intense strokes deep within her. Gabrielle quaked, her body enveloped in the raw energy, the wonder of the electricity racing through every limb. She felt more of her wetness leaking from her, pooling beneath her as Gregory worked his tongue at the sensitive apex of her thighs. He struck a punishing pace, his head bobbing furiously as he devoured her, his moans vibrating against her hot skin. She writhed in pleasure, twisting his hair tightly between her fingers, as her legs trembled with the force of his mouth against her.

Gregory was like a man in a trance. He could not believe that he was worshipping his new bride, a slave to her taste, her sleek wetness, the feel of her skin and the smell of her hair permeated his senses in a kaleidoscope of emotion. He sensed her approaching release; her hips began to rock with each tongue stroke and, whether she was aware or not, she pressed his face tightly to her as her fingers clutched his hair. He smiled against her, and looped his left arm across both her hips, pinning her to the mattress more firmly. He buried his tongue even farther against the sensitive bundle at her apex, with a gentle intensity that made Gabrielle's legs twitch of their own accord on either side of him. Slowly, he drew his right hand down between her legs to tease at her opening. Just as his tongue quickened, he plunged one finger into her, curling it and stroking in time with his tongue.

One...two... three more strokes and he felt Gabrielle's inner muscles tighten. With one final flick of his tongue, Gabrielle cried a long, shuddering moan, her body tensing against him. She felt herself seized in torturous ecstasy. Oh God, she'd never felt like this: fractured and mindless and utterly at Gregory's mercy. She chased the wave of her pleasure for what felt like an eternity before her cry died down and she sank, trembling, into the mattress.

"Welcome back my love," Gregory said, as he rose again, positioning himself above her. Gabrielle could only manage a small moan, smiling, as she panted in the afterglow of her very first orgasm.

She slowly opened her eyes and met his own which were lit as if on fire. He nibbled against her neck and swept kisses around her bosom and painfully taut nipples.

"Are you ready for me?" Gregory asked, his voice low and growling.

Gabrielle spread her legs as wide as they'd go, welcoming the slide of his massive manhood against her glistening opening. "I am so very...very...ready for you, Gregory." Gabrielle kissed him, sweeping her tongue across his perfect teeth and around his tongue, catching the remnants of her wetness on his lips.

Gregory pulled gently away as he propped Gabrielle up higher on the bed, cradling her head until it rested against a feathery soft pillow, before laying himself fully atop her. "I am delighted to hear that madam wife."

Gabrielle stroked his belly as he leaned his head back and groaned. This encouraged her to reach for his manhood, tentatively at first and then more urgently. She wrapped both hands around his massive manhood shocked by the smoothness of it, like hot marble beneath her working fingers. She slid her hands up and down his length as he bucked against her grip, a strangled gasp escaping his lips.

"Oh God, Gabrielle. You must stop. Oh God, I shall explode."

She stroked him once more, firmly along the full length of his shaft as his face contorted into blissful agony. But he would not release yet, he could not until he'd sunk himself as deeply as he could inside her. He grasped each of her hands again, kissing them gently before placing them on his shoulders. Gregory met her eyes with his own, blazing with need, and she knew in that moment that he was holding himself back with every shred of restraint he possessed.

She arced against him, brushing her nipples against his chest, grinning wickedly. Gregory's shallow panting and wide eyes foretold of his hard core on the precipice of bursting. He swept his hips up and down, rubbing himself along the full length of her, still slick and hot and ripe for him. With each sweep, Gabrielle's head leaned back exposing her long white neck. Gregory kissed his wife's beautiful neck as he swept against her again.

Gabrielle whispered, "More, Gregory more. I want…I need… more."

"Gabrielle, look at me." Gregory's voice was hoarse. "Look at me. I want more, too. I need more. But there may be some…discomfort…at first. Only at first. I'd never want to hurt you. What do you want Gabrielle?"

Gabrielle opened her eyes again, mesmerized as she looked deep into his eyes. She smiled, touched by his concern for her. Gregory nipped at her bosom and asked again softly, "Tell me what you want."

Gabrielle, through her veiled eyes, looked back into his with a new certainly settling over her. "I want you inside me, Gregory. Please. Please. *Plea—*"

Gabrielle screamed at his first thrust inside her, though as much from the full pleasure of it as the momentary pain. There was discomfort, a sharp-edged pain for a moment, and Gregory carefully stilled inside her to give her time to adjust. As soon as the pain passed, all she could think about was the size of him, stretching and filling her. She longed for more and began to move up and down against him, wrapping her long legs around his waist as she did so. Gregory took her cue and began slow, steady, and deep thrusts in and out of her, but as Gabrielle continued to moan, he could not control himself any longer.

His restraint snapped and he moaned her name over and over again as he struck a more demanding pace, pounding hard into her as he felt her inner muscles clench and unclench around him. God, he was going to lose himself in this woman. And to his surprise, Gabrielle matched his thrusts with the same vigor and need as his own, rocking her hips up to meet his devastating pounding and taking him deep. He speared his fingers through her hair, gripping tightly as he pulled her head back, causing her to arc beneath him. Her breasts bounced with each hammering thrust, and he couldn't resist lowering his mouth to clamp around her nipple once more. Gabrielle screamed his name as he sucked her hard, consuming her with tongue and teeth; the relentless rhythm of Gregory's hard body pumping and filling her, her wetness dripping down her legs, her desperate high-pitched whimpers, the bounce of her breast in his mouth, made him swell and finally explode. He released her nipple as he plunged his full length deep inside her one last time, a strangled growl escaping as his orgasm barreled through him and Gabrielle, too, found her second, quivering release. It felt like an eternity in this bliss, but finally, both spent, they fell together back to earth.

AUSPICIOUS STARTS AND STOPS

*D*ays flew into weeks as Gabrielle was fast adjusting to her new life at Ramsgate. Every morning, she stirred briefly as her husband lay a gentle kiss on her forehead before he left to attend his ducal duties. Gabrielle, an early riser always, was surprised by how much earlier her husband would start his day. In the first few days of their marriage, Gabrielle would sabotage Gregory's efforts for an early start by using her newfound seductive powers to entice him back to their bed. Gregory soon caught onto her designs and ensured that she was so exhausted by his lovemaking every night that she merely smiled and sighed when he left their bed come the early morning. Gabrielle and Gregory were perfectly content to play this game back and forth, their laughing eyes displaying the passion that fired so easily between them.

Once Gregory left for his work, Gabrielle's maidservant

Annie arrived and drew a bath, helping her dress once Gabrielle was clean. As a duchess, Gabrielle was expected to dress every day. Before their marriage, Gabrielle had been fitted by the best designers for an entirely new wardrobe and attending accessories befitting a lady of her station. Gabrielle had never wanted anything in her life before the duke, but this extravagance was an entirely new way of living. Although it could be tedious, Gabrielle was humble enough to appreciate her good fortune.

One crisp fall morning, Gabrielle decided to ride before dressing for the day. Gabrielle preferred morning rides to afternoon which would then require her to re-dress and bathe several times in one day, taking up precious hours that she instead used to read, or walk the grounds. She was slowly learning her way around the property, introducing herself to the servants and workers there as she happened upon them.

The first time she came upon Gregory during his morning work, he was stunned to see her. It had been a beautiful fall day and Gabrielle wore her white ruffle shirt that tied at the neck, with her custom-made breeches. It had never occurred to Gregory that his wife would continue dressing like a boy on their grounds. He assumed that she would dress appropriately and ride side saddle at their estate, especially when she was hosting her family or visitors, as was the case today.

Gabrielle had ridden hard and fast across the meadow towards Gregory, who was working with his agricultural engineer, when he caught sight of Gabrielle on her white thoroughbred racing over, her hair streaming behind. She stopped perfectly and precisely at their feet and jumped nimbly off her horse, stunning both men. Gregory recovered first and said, "Ian, let's take a break, shall we? Please return to the main house and have some breakfast."

Ian who continued to stare in shock at Gabrielle, finally answered with a bow. "Yes, milord. My lady," he mumbled as he whisked off to his horse and buggy, heading back to the main house, not daring to glance back.

"Gabrielle, what in the hell do you think you are doing, wearing nearly nothing, and riding astride for all to see? I can well imagine what the groomsmen thought when they saw you this morning!"

Gabrielle who had been smiling brightly until that moment, frowned as she patted her legs and then promptly lifted her chin. "Gregory, you said that I could do exactly as I pleased here at *our* estate. I have always worn britches to ride when I am at home! I would never do so when there are guests, but our staff certainly knows that this is my preferred dress so I can ride as unimpeded as any man can. I am sorry that this displeases you, but I have no intention of changing my ways." The pink in her cheeks deepened, though not from shame.

Gregory looked at her and could not help but smile. His wife was so beautiful in the sunlight, her skin glistening from the excursion of her ride, and her eyes alight with indignation. He walked over to her and touched her cheek, gently pushing away an errant blonde curl. Gabrielle smiled hesitantly, trying to determine if the storm had passed, as she wrapped her arms around his neck.

"Good morning my lord," she said, kissing him. Gregory gathered her up in his arms, walked over to the full shade of the willow tree, placing her carefully under its long branches onto the moss skirt.

"Good morning my wife," he smiled as he gently began undoing the buttons on her breeches. Gabrielle, catching his intention, eagerly undid the bow at her collar, letting her bare breasts fall out of the fabric, ready to be worshipped.

Several weeks after Gregory and Gabrielle had wed, Jacques Martin had scheduled a meeting with Gregory and the top investors of the London waterworks project at the Lions Club. Among the group included the top financiers, dignitaries, and politicians of the era including James Rittenhouse, who was an advisor on the project as well.

The project was in its last stages of completion and there were many questions about who would be appointed the custodian of the new sewer and water systems, and whether to allow it to fall under the purview of Parliament and the people or instead allow it to be completely privatized. Gregory and Jacques believed that while it should sit under the supervision of Parliament, and hence the people of England, it was also important that its supervision be balanced by good financiers, and knowledgeable engineers available for the work as independent contractors for hire.

Having failed in his previous attempts to discredit Jacques Martin, Norwood had been working not-so-secretly behind the scenes on a scheme to buy the votes from those in Parliament who were susceptible, which would allow him to become the principal custodian of the new system. Even though Norwood had been removed from any project details in its development thanks to Jacques Martin and Joseph Bazelguette, Norwood was relentless in his pursuit to neutralize his foes and get control of the project so he could exact his punishment when the moment presented itself. Norwood was close to being rewarded for his manipulations and machinations. With the support of his father-in-law, Earl Sinclair, Norwood's plan was to be named as custodian and oversee the newly upgraded water system. In naming Norwood as custodian, the Earl would of course provide a permanent role for his son-in-law, and win Norwood full vindication after suffering the humiliation that the project's founders had so unceremoniously inflicted upon him.

Gregory and Jacques, both warned of Norwood's efforts, had rallied their support via James Rittenhouse and the powerful constituents of their parliamentary friends and associates.

James and Gregory had just met with Jacques Martin and Joseph Bazelguette to review the final proposal for the custodianship of the London waterworks system which would be presented to Parliament the following week. The men were satisfied with their proposal and believed that once heard, Parliament would see the truth and necessity of a split supervision between government and independent contractors, both held to the high standards that were required for its sustainable success. They were adamant that this meant the exclusion of the Earl and Norwood, due to their obvious conflict of interest. Many in Parliament agreed with the plan given the Earl and his son-in-law's ruthless reputations, but there were a few who were being tempted to vote against the proposal.

White's Club was busy on the evening of their meeting, where the group had gathered after their tour of the underground ducts. A fire burned brightly, though its light did not quite reach the darkest corners of the salon. Jacques Martin had just finished his brandy and stood, as Gregory and James also rose to wish him a good evening. As Gregory and Jacques shook hands, the older man placed a hand on his son-in-law's shoulder.

"How goes it with my spitfire daughter?" Jacques smiled kindly as Gregory drew a breath in, some color rising in his cheeks.

Gregory cleared his throat before he spoke, "Well, Sir Martin. I have no complaints."

Jacques smiled shrewdly, pleased with the genuine affection he detected in Gregory's tone. "Good, I am satisfied. This union is indeed built on a strong foundation.

Gregory, please wish my daughter well. Her mother and I will visit soon."

And with that, Jacques took his leave. Gregory and James remained, leaving the two younger men to linger over their scotches. It had been a long day and the hour of closing at White's was nearly upon them. James and Gregory clinked their glasses together in a final toast before departing for the evening.

"Well, well Gregory," James said, leaning back in his chair, "Marriage does seem to suit you as much as it does your beautiful wife." He rested his elbows on the armchair as he smiled at his good friend.

"I cannot disagree with you, my friend." Gregory smiled back and continued, "I wholeheartedly recommend the institution of marriage. So, tell me," he said slyly, "How is the lovely lady Patrice these days?"

James sighed deeply, "Ah, Gregory, lovely, that she is!" James' smile changed into a frown as he peered into his empty glass and sighed. "But as you know I am a confirmed bachelor. One of us needs to honor our promise."

"Bullocks, James." Gregory set his glass down firmly and leaned forward with an earnest look on his face. "You cannot believe that you must remain a bachelor to fulfill some ridiculous promise we made when we were disenchanted boys?"

James looked away, gripping the worn leather armrests of his chair. Gregory knew he should stop, but could not help but press his friend, knowing something of James' heart.

"James, what is it? What makes you so determined to avoid marrying a beautiful woman whom you admire, and for whom you hold quite a bit of affection?"

Gregory had long noticed James' regard for Patrice and in turn the young lady's own interest in Gregory's friend. Their attraction was like electricity, like that charge in the air Gregory experienced with Gabrielle. Gregory could not help but smile at the thought of a match between James and Patrice.

James and Gregory had been close, like brothers always, having both lost their families in their youth. But where Gregory had fond memories of his father, the Duke, James did not have the benefit of that memory and knowledge. On the contrary, James had been raised by a wicked woman who spent her entire marriage cuckolding her husband. James swore he would never allow himself to marry and be vulnerable like his father. James stretched, composing his thoughts carefully before he spoke again. "Gregory, I am content in my bachelorhood as I would never be able to be in marriage, even to Patrice Corchoran."

James leaned back, but Gregory would not take the hint. "James, you will regret her when she finally does take a husband."

"Have you heard that she is to be married?" James tried to feign nonchalance, but Gregory was not fooled.

Gregory smirked, before he answered, "No, not yet

man, but it is inevitable and when that time comes you will need to be prepared. James," Gregory leaned forward in hushed tones, "don't be held by a past that you had no control over. Patrice is nothing like your—" Gregory stopped himself in time from speaking out loud James' mother's name, just as he met his friend's eyes which were now filled with ire. Gregory sighed. "James…Patrice is unique, like Gabrielle; she is not selfish or mean-spirited. And she holds affection for you."

James was determined to change the subject at any cost. He stood quickly and smiled. "Gregory, my friend you are truly besotted by your wife. I congratulate you on defying the odds and discovering your love match, but please let's not ever broach this subject of marriage again where I am concerned. My life is far more complicated than yours, Duke. I bid you adieu," he said curtly.

Gregory sipped the last of his whiskey as he watched James leave, thinking about his friend and why the idea of love and marriage was so frightening to him, recollecting his own reluctance to marry. Yes, he remembered it well, though he hoped that love would one day warm his young friend's frozen heart.

LAUNCHES AND BETRAYAL

*F*all was just beginning to wane when Gabrielle was delighted to receive word that Patrice would visit for a full two weeks at Ramsgate, during which time Gregory and Gabrielle were to host their first ball as a married couple. Of course, Patrice was among the first to respond to the invitation and was a welcome helper as the newly-wedded Stalwards made their official launch into society as husband and wife. Gregory deferred all the details of their debut ball to his wife, and Gabrielle, though pleased to have such authority, felt the pressure of ensuring their launch into society was handled perfectly. Patrice's presence would help calm her and provide the right distraction so that Gabrielle could begin to enjoy the process of putting the event together.

Gabrielle had missed her best friend's company and

could hardly wait to regale Patrice with stories of her developing responsibilities as Duchess of Montrose. Patrice, meanwhile, had been in London proper all season long with several dapper young men vying for her attention. Patrice's parents were quite frustrated with their daughter for not choosing among her many suitors one good husband, but Patrice, so like Gabrielle in matters of the heart, was not easily swayed by just any suitor.

And of course, there was the matter of James Rittenhouse who remained inscrutable in his manner towards Patrice, which grew much more reserved than when they first danced together at Gabrielle's debut ball. Patrice in turn was careful to never show James any favoritism as she was unsure if he would reject it. Long had Patrice been convinced that James would likely never marry of his own accord, but that would not stop her from secretly hoping that she could turn his mind.

As circumstances would have, James and Patrice spent very little time together and were never alone. And although Patrice knew they had forged a deep connection, she also knew well that James resisted it. Theirs was an intimate and dangerous dance that she feared would end in her own tears and regret. But she could no sooner turn her hopes and dreams away from James as she could avoid the sun. Patrice sighed and turned her attention eagerly to visiting Gabrielle. This trip with Gabrielle would give Patrice a respite from her complicated situation and hopefully afford her time to plan how to handle the brooding, elusive James Rittenhouse.

After a day spent preparing for the ball, Gabrielle and Patrice decided to ride to the sea and enjoy the early fall weather. They basked in the late day sun and even took off their shoes to walk in the gentle surf. It felt like old times to Gabrielle, before her debut and before her wedding, and she relished feeling like a girl again.

"Patrice," she asked after some time "the men won't be back until late tonight, so we are in no rush to return. Let's walk some more?"

Patrice happily agreed. She had many questions about her new marriage and this was a perfect time to fill her curiosity. "So, Gabrielle, I want details..." Patrice said teasingly.

Gabrielle smiled, knowing where the direction of their conversation was likely headed. "Well, come on now," Patrice nudged, "I want to hear how you have so quickly turned into this content new bride after so many years of clashing with your husband?"

Gabrielle sighed deeply and smiled back at Patrice. "I am embarrassed to tell you...Patrice, I am quite surprised by my husband. As much as I thought I knew the boy and the man, there was more to him that I underestimated. I have observed his strength of character, a tremendous amount of integrity, the humility to work alongside his tenants rather than above them, and yes, he has made me quite…. satisfied to be his wife." Gabrielle tried to hide a smile from her inquisitive friend to no avail.

"Gabrielle, I do believe you are in love!" Patrice squealed. When Gabrielle turned away without immediate reply, Patrice spun Gabrielle to face her. "Oh, my goodness, you *are* in love!" Patrice clapped her hands in joy. Gabrielle neither confirmed nor denied, although a hint of worry clouded her bright eyes. Patrice immediately discerned this and reached for her friend. "What is it, Gabrielle? All is well is it not?"

"Yes, of course, all is well. It's just—" Gabrielle struggled to find the words. "It's just that he has never said he loves me. I never expected that those words would hold importance to me, but suddenly it seems necessary. It's so silly, really." Gabrielle shrugged. "It's not that I am unhappy…It's just that… I find myself wondering about his feelings for me."

"Gabrielle, anyone with two eyes can see how the man looks at you. It is positively scandalous. Of course, he has warm feelings for you!" Patrice hugged Gabrielle's shoulders.

"Patrice, one thing I learned is that two people can have a powerful… reaction… to one another but that doesn't mean it is love."

Patrice wanted to ask her friend so much more but felt that this might be crossing an unspoken barrier into Gabrielle's heart, a space reserved for Gregory. The young women made their way back to the estate in contemplative silence.

A week later, and finally, the long-awaited launch of the London Waterworks finally arrived. The launch itself was quite the spectacle with a brass band and flags waving in the hands of the spectators crowding the streets to witness such vast innovation; indeed, Gregory thought, the atmosphere was more akin to a carnival than a serious scientific launch. At the heart of the activity, the men most responsible for the new system—Bazelguette, Jacques Martin, Gregory, and James Rittenhouse—assisted with the actual first documented and official release of the new water flow.

Gregory and James worked alongside some of the day laborers. Having immediately removed their long black coats and hat, the gentlemen certainly did not look the part of lords of the upper class as they all lent their bodies to the physical task of directing the masons, welders, and workers as they fit the last large pipe into the ground below the bridge of London Square.

Gregory and James dug their heels into the rocky soil as they leaned their shoulders on the massive piping. A single cry of *"heave!"* and the men in perfect synchronicity managed to move the pipe inch by inch until it finally slipped into the correct position. The welders and masons on hand quickly sealed any gaps between the new piping and the enormous plug.

As the final sparks flew, then sizzled to black, the crowd roared. It was done! Now all that remained was to wait for the water to flow. Everyone waited with bated breath for the sound of rushing water through the piping. Within a few moments, they were rewarded as the first gurgles were heard, followed by a sound of rushing water. The launch was a success!

Gregory and James smiled as Jacques Martin put his arms around the younger men and laughed. In that moment, Gregory felt something sharp in his chest, knowing instantly it was not of a physical nature, but he nevertheless felt it keenly. Indeed, the gnawing feeling he realized was regret that Gabrielle was not standing among them to share in the joy of this moment. All he could think of was how proud she would be, and how deserving she too was to share in the glory and joy of this moment of completion to a project that had been painstaking to her father, and herself for years.

That morning, he kissed her softly as he left for the day, and she seemed sound asleep, though he knew she was not; her disappointment at being left behind was too strong. It was painful for her to miss this moment, even though women were not expected to attend events like this, particularly because of the harsh, and exacting conditions involved in its inception. But it mattered not. For the first time, Gregory seemed to understand the frustration that his wife felt at being nearly invisible in something so great as this—especially when she was so worthy of respect.

Just then, James Rittenhouse grabbed his arm, rousing him out of his somber thoughts. "Come, Gregory, we must celebrate this—let's go to White's for an evening of drink." Gregory smiled and followed the party, intending to stay only for a short time so he could return to his wife.

White's was indeed bustling and many more drinks than Gregory anticipated were poured and toasted over. Night had long since fallen when Gregory, eager to return home, rose to leave. As he did so, his eyes locked with those of Norwood, who stared back with obvious hatred.

"Gregory," James said at his shoulder, "let it pass. The man is as green with envy as his heart is black with hatred. It is incredibly shameless that he would be here tonight, but God forbid anyone turn away the Earl's son-in-law." And then, seeing Gregory's attention had not wavered, James asked, "Lord Gregory, might I ask for lodging at your home this evening? The idea of taking my carriage back alone is not at all compelling."

Gregory broke his gaze with Norwood at last. "Why do I doubt that you are feeling lonely for *my* company this evening, and likely more concerned that I might meet with some unexpected injury to my person? But yes, I would be delighted to have you stay with us this evening." Gregory smiled slyly at the thought of James and Patrice finding themselves unexpectedly thrown together for the day.

The carriage ride was relatively short given the late

hour, and they arrived at Montrose Estate in short order. James watched his friend eagerly make way to his bedroom and smiled.

Gregory opened the bedchamber door softly, uncertain if Gabrielle would be awake or not. And try as she might, Gabrielle had indeed finally fallen asleep in her lounge chair by the fire. She was awakened with a soft kiss on her brow.

"My dear," Gregory murmured, "you are enchanting in the firelight."

Gabrielle lifted her arms sleepily to wrap them around Gregory's neck. Gregory gently unclasped her hands whispering, "I need a bath before I can come to your bed. But I beg of you, please be ready for me." Gabrielle closed her eyes and swooned at his passionate whispers.

Given the late hour, Gregory drew his own bath and so it was some time before he settled into the steaming water and quickly soaped his body. He ducked his head under the water, rising quickly as he brushed his wet hair back from his eyes. Suddenly, Gabrielle's soft hands on his shoulders startled him and he made to rise from the water to face her.

"No, you don't sir." Gabrielle gently pushed him back into the tub. She let go of his shoulders, trailing one finger down his arm as she stepped around the side of the tub to face him. Gregory noted with a soft moan that she was already naked, and the candlelight gleamed off every curve, from the sweep of her breasts down to the shadowed patch of hair between her legs. Smiling, she stepped into the sudsy water and lowered herself as she straddled him. She had tied her golden hair up loosely, so several soft curls were left to fall on her full and upright breasts. Just the sight of her, Gregory found, was enough to stir his loins to full attention.

"You surprise me every day and night my dear," Gregory sighed as he ran his hands down her back, grabbing her buttocks beneath the water. Gabrielle leaned in, bracing her hands on the side of the tub, and kissed him deeply. Below the water, she could feel Gregory's erection between her thighs, and she teased him by rubbing the tip of him along the sleek folds of her opening. He groaned into the kiss and attempted to seat himself in her, but she resisted, enjoying taunting him.

"I hope I am a happy surprise," Gabrielle smiled seductively as she ran her tongue across his lips, nipping his lower lip gently. She released her left hand from the edge of the tub and slid it down to grip his shaft fully. Gregory shuddered, throwing his head back as she worked his sleek full length with her slender fingers, the steady up and down driving his hips to unconscious thrusting. Then, without warning, Gabrielle removed her hand and quickly slid onto his hard length fully, seating herself so that every glorious inch of him was inside her. Gregory groaned out loud with the suddenness of it and Gabrielle gripped his shoulders, throwing her head back as she shuddered. Sweat trickled down her shoulders, slid in between her breasts which rocked in time with her hips just in front of Gregory's face.

Releasing her buttocks, Gregory cupped her breasts, bringing her to him so he could tease her nipples. Sucking one breast into his mouth, he flicked the other nipple playfully, the way he'd learned she liked, eliciting helpless little squeaks each time his tongue passed over her hardened peaks. Gabrielle could hardly contain the heat that coiled within her, how Gregory filled her so completely that every vein, every limb, was claimed. His mouth moved to the other breast, clamping hard on her sensitive nipple, and she nearly climaxed as he rolled his tongue across her.

Instead of pounding into her, Gabrielle deliberately held Gregory fully inside her and began rotating her hips instead, first in slow circles and then faster and faster. His phallus, so deep inside her, hit spots she didn't know her body possessed and the senseless pleasure of it drove her on.

"Oh, Gregory," she gasped, gripping his shoulders. Gregory released her breasts, sensing Gabrielle was nearing her release. With eyes closed and head thrown back, she was using him, he realized, riding him hard and lost in the electricity of her own body. He smiled, watching her take her pleasure from him, rocking harder and harder on his near bursting member.

"That's right, Gabrielle," he murmured, "That's right. Take me, my love."

Her breaths came in little gasps now riding him so fast water sloshed over the sides of the tub. Grinning, feeling his release close he slid a hand beneath the water and held two fingers against her delicate bundle of nerves so she rubbed against them with each circle of her hips. She was on the edge, he could feel it, the tense inner walls of her clamping tightly around him, the bobbing of her sweat-glistened breasts in front of him, the graceful arc of her neck joyously thrown back.

"Take me, Gabrielle..." he whispered once more, and then she screamed her climax.

"I'm taking you...I'm taking all of you...Oh, Gregory!" She pumped her hips furiously, the strength of her orgasm barreling through them both, as water sloshed the tiled floor. Gregory laughed huskily as his breath caught in his throat. Never had he felt so free and alive, so willing to surrender everything, as he did with this woman of his dreams. His climax engulfed him at last, the strength of it surprising him as he slammed into her.

"Gab—ri—elle!" he cried, as each pulse released another wave of pleasure. As her orgasm abated, she fell against him, exhausted but smiling. The bathwater had begun to cool, so Gregory lifted his sleepy wife out of the tub and wrapped the large white towel around her.

"Hmmm," she sighed sleepily, allowing her husband to gently warm and dry her.

"Feel good, angel?" Gregory wrapped the towel around Gabrielle and swept her off her feet towards their bed.

"Marvelous, my lord," Gabrielle murmured. As he laid Gabrielle down on the bed, his gaze smoldered, his eyes scanning her golden skin, her hair, and the beautiful curls between her long legs.

"Good," he whispered. Leaning his head down to her crowning center, he lifted her buttocks as he wrapped her legs around his neck. He gently and reverently sank between her thighs with soft gentle kisses and strokes of his lips and tongue. Gabrielle gasped and raised her hips to meet him, the slow lazy sweeps of his tongue wetting her fully and sending shivers of pleasure down her spine. He groaned against her, the deep vibrations along with his expert tongue sending her closer to another release. She was nearly there already, arcing her back and pressing herself to his tongue, when he disappeared from between her legs.

Gabrielle had just enough time to glance up, puzzled, before Gregory yanked her to the edge of the bed, propping her legs up against his chest and gripping her buttocks as he stood over her. She smiled as she felt his erection again, pleasantly surprised. Without waiting, Gregory pushed into her in one slow, torturous thrust, a husky moan escaping his lips.

"You feel heavenly," he whispered, sliding out and back in again.

"As do you, my lord," Gabrielle breathed. She wanted him to go faster, wanted him to pound her hard, but the agonizing tenderness of his movements built within her nonetheless.

"Say that again," Gregory grunted, pumping her again with agonizing slowness.

"My lord," she moaned.

"Again." This time, when he slid into her, she could feel him swelling, his girth stretching her with torturous pleasure.

"My lord," Gabrielle panted. His thrust was harder this time, pushing her farther on the mattress so he had to grip her buttocks and yank her back. He released her, sliding his hands along her hips until the broad press of his hands pinned her, pressing on her lower belly.

"My lord," she moaned, closing her eyes. She could not move her hips but reached her hands above her head to tangle in the sheets. He grunted as he pounded into her so hard, she would have slid farther onto the bed were he not gripping her so tightly. Gabrielle opened her eyes and locked with Gregory's dark gaze. Oh, then his restraint snapped and when he hammered into her, she cried out again and again, the fast slaps of his skin to hers driving them both to the edge.

"Again," Gregory commanded, grunting with each thrust into her core.

"My lord!" she cried, "My lord … my lord … *my lord*!" Her last cry dissolved into a mindless scream as Gregory found his release, pumping into her with such abandon that Gabrielle quickly climaxed with him, bowing off the mattress with the power of their orgasms, her gushing wetness seeping around him as he spent himself in her.

When at last they were both sated, Gregory climbed under the sheets and pulled Gabrielle close to him so her back rested against his chest.

"So," Gabrielle said, a sly grin sliding across her face, "it seems the project launched successfully?"

"It was a wonder," Gregory said, "When we finally heard the water flowing, it was a victorious moment." He propped himself onto his elbow and looked down at Gabrielle with serious eyes. "Gabrielle, you should have been there. You should have been by my side, enjoying the success of the moment. I am sorry." Gregory kissed her brow.

Gabrielle sighed sadly. "Perhaps now you can understand why I am so frustrated by the rules of society as they relate to women especially. It is only with help from those in power that we can make change."

"I promise you, Gabrielle, that is the last time you will not be my side in any victory or defeat. You are my wife." Gregory was solemn as Gabrielle met his lips in a sweet kiss.

Having finally settled in his room, James found he could not sleep as the events of the evening turned over in his mind. Why was Norwood at the celebration for the waterworks project? In some way it was a good sign that he may have finally resigned himself to the fact that he was forever in the background where he'd been banished, quite rightly. And when the custodianship of the waterworks had been turned over to Jacques Martin's choice, thanks to James Rittenhouse's efforts within Parliament, Norwood's last attempt to extract some measure of control was squelched permanently.

Perhaps Norwood's presence at the men's club on this night was his way to move forward with the new order of esteemed engineers in London and put the past behind him. But James doubted this even as he sought to rationalize Norwood's presence. The man was a manipulative coward and the fact that he showed up to the closing night of the project from which he had been forced to remove himself, did not sit well with James. He never trusted Norwood and never would. Something was amiss.

James stretched as he removed his cravat and unbuttoned his shirt, rolling up the sleeves of his shirt. It was no use. He would not be able to sleep tonight. He quietly let himself out of his bedroom and proceeded to make his way to the kitchen where he hoped to find some food and drink.

Patrice had just finished her glass of milk when the kitchen doors opened and James Rittenhouse, the object of her musings, walked in. Patrice almost dropped her glass, so shocked by James' presence she was.

"What are you doing here?" Patrice's tone of voice

emerged with more annoyance than surprise. James was equally startled to find Patrice in the kitchen, wearing nothing but her white lace chemise, and thin matching robe, barefoot, her long dark hair reaching her waist.

His state of dishabille, barefoot and with his shirt untucked and open to reveal the dark, curly hair on his muscular chest gave Patrice pause, too. She stood abruptly and walked to the farm sink, taking time to compose herself as she washed the cup. James watched her move, her hair skimming the top of her buttocks as it cast a shadow over the round firmness there. When she turned to face him, James saw the fire in her eyes and the blush on her cheeks.

"Gregory asked me to escort him home so in the morning we can look over some of the paperwork we will need to submit to Parliament next week," James said, feigning a nonchalant shrug, "I was hungry and thought I would find something to satisfy my craving. It seems I have." His eyes twinkled and locked with Patrice's own.

Patrice pulled her shoulders back as she raised her chin in a show of confidence, unwittingly pushing her taut nipples, free of a corset, against the soft lacy satin so James could just barely glimpse the soft chestnut shade of their peaks. When she realized where his gaze went, Patrice quickly pulled her robe closed and started to walk towards the door, brushing by James as she did so.

James stopped her by placing a hand on her shoulder. "Patrice," he murmured, "I won't bite you, as tempting as the thought is. Sit with me for a bit. I am still celebrating our success tonight. Keep me company."

Patrice found she could not refuse him, something vulnerable in the depths of his voice stirring her heart. She faced him as calmly as she could and asked him about the evening. He was in a talkative mood and shared the details of the long day. They both sat at the kitchen table and the hour passed quickly. Patrice laughed at James' description of Gregory and him working on the pipes at the London site.

"Oh, so is that where you got so dirty?" She reached out smiling and touched his cheek where he had missed cleaning a light smudge of dirt that still showed. James stopped breathing as their gaze held. Patrice drew back her long fingers, licking her forefinger before placing it back onto the smudged spot and gently rubbing it clean.

"There, all clean." Patrice smiled up at him, her blush deepening. James' willpower could not withstand her gentle onslaught of kindness. He reached to cup her face gently in his hands. Patrice was ready and willing to share a kiss with him, her lips parted, her eyes brilliant and dancing in the candlelight.

James began to bend his head to her when common sense wielded its inconvenient head. He could not under any circumstances ever be found in such a compromising position with Patrice. Willing himself, he pulled away from her, watching Patrice's crestfallen face. She held his eyes for a moment longer, filled with regret and deep longing.

When it was clear he was not going to follow through on the promise of the moment, Patrice rose in anger. She spun on her heel and walked towards the door before turning back to face him.

"Coward," Patrice whispered bitterly, before striding out of the kitchen, leaving him deflated in her wake. James slumped into the chair, knowing that Patrice spoke the truth about him.

BALLS AND THEIR FIREWORKS

*T*he week before the ball passed in a blur, as all were busy with plans for the Stalward's debut event. Patrice helped Gabrielle manage the details of the event of the season, occasionally assuming control when Gabrielle, dizzy from her meetings with the household staff, local grocer and butcher, florists, and chefs, the string octet, and finally waved off any more decisions with an exhausted sigh. The household maidservants ran on call day and night, working tirelessly to showcase the Stalward house at its very best for London's finest.

Gregory had convinced James to stay on with the rest of the Martin and Corchoran families until the ball. The lively party spent their evenings engaged in long talks, walks, and card games. One night, Gabrielle and Gregory suggested the group play a game of charades. They all had a rousing good time. Jacques and his wife exchanged happy smiles as they heard Gregory laugh out loud at his wife's irreverent rendition of England's current king and queen, who fortunately were not present to witness the teasing.

Patrice clasped her hands over her mouth as her giggles turned to rapturous laughter at Gabrielle's hilarious impersonations, as well, unaware that James Rittenhouse still studied her every chance he could. He was, he had to conclude, completely caught off guard by the woman. He watched Patrice and Gabrielle laugh and tease one another, Patrice's bosom rising beautifully with every excited breath. Occasionally, their eyes met, and Patrice's smile would freeze as she watched the burn in her admirer's eyes. Electricity ran between the two, and only when Gregory discreetly cleared his throat before calling out to his friend, did James eventually rouse himself from his desirous stupor.

"James, you alone remain the only one to not have played his hand at some charade tonight. Care to take a turn?" smiled Gregory already knowing the likely response of his friend.

James calmly responded, "I wouldn't dare try my hand at this, particularly following such a performance. Far better to let us end this game on a high note." All laughed, enjoying the relaxed atmosphere of true friends and family. Fellowship, lighthearted banter, and the long passionate looks between the young couples when they thought no one the wiser, made for good sport for Jacques and Elizabeth Martin, and their dearest friends Thomas and Angelica

Corchoran, who noted the affection that bloomed between their daughter and James Rittenhouse.

Finally, the long-awaited ball was at hand. The tables were set, candles lit, and flowers adorned every corner of Montrose Estate as far as the eye could see. A musical trio played a tender melody as the guests arrived. The servants had spent a week preparing the crystals, China dishes, and silver so that all glistened brightly by the candlelight and reflections in the mirrors which adorned the expansive rooms. The ballroom shone in particular glory as the sconces in the magnificent hall were each lit, while the mirrored walls bounced their light over the party assembled.

The hosts for the evening were in their finest form indeed. Lord Gregory wore his white coat and tails for the occasion and his wife had thoughtfully procured a dashing boutonniere that matched the orchids draped in her beautifully coiffed hair. Piled high in Grecian fashion, Gabrielle's curls cascaded down and around her fair shoulder. Gabrielle had been reviewing the final details with staff as James and Patrice met her at the top of the stairs leading to the ballroom. Gabrielle then took James' left arm, and Patrice at his right, and so the trio descended.

Gabrielle just then caught the look in her husband's glistening eye and smiled that secret smile, letting him know she remembered their lovemaking just hours earlier. Gregory had known early in the day that he was facing a long and exhausting evening. He had therefore resolved to temper his arousal and appetite for his bride before the ball. Gabrielle had been extremely distracted with the details of the ball, but relented to Gregory's persistent efforts and knowing the pleasure and joy it always gave her, they spent a vigorous hour with Gabrielle's legs wrapped around his waist, the glow of which still shone in Gabrielle's peachy pink cheeks, which needed no other enhancement.

James moved towards his friend and whispered, "Gregory you look as if you are ready to carry your wife off over your shoulder."

Gregory's spell temporarily broken, replied with his answering smile. "James, my friend, I envy your ability to be so restrained when in the presence of your siren who beckons you."

James' smile turned to a frown at Gregory's gentle rebuke. James would have to be a blind man to not notice that Patrice did look particularly exquisite this evening. Her gown clung to her figure in all the right places and her bosom looked as if it would fall out of the tightly closed bodice. Her hair was coiled in a low bun at her nape, with gentle tendrils falling to her collarbone and back. He longed to reach for one the curls and breathe in her perfume. Just as he thought to ask a dance from her, Patrice was approached by one of the Sinclair's distant relations, an obvious fop of a boy. Patrice extended her hand which was happily received by the young man as they made their way to the dance floor.

"Missed yet another opportunity my friend," Gregory said as he moved to take his leave and greet more of his guests who had just arrived. James stared back with a blank face, though he was annoyed by his friend's teasing remarks.

The ball was a tremendous success. The champagne flowed and the orchestra had the attendees on their feet dancing under the candlelight in the ballroom and outside to the veranda where the guests whirled and twirled under the stars. Everyone was in attendance, including the officious Earl Sinclair, his daughter Clara, and her boorish husband, Alfred Norwood. Regardless of the antipathy between the Stalwards and Norwood, they would always have to include one another in events such as these that were intended for most of London society.

It had been a perfect evening and the wine flowed freely as the company was happily engaged in dance and gaiety. The orchestra was superb and even the crotchetier members of society found themselves tapping their toes to the music. Gabrielle and Gregory led the assembly in yet another dance, smiling as they twirled the dance floor to a waltz.

In the meantime, Patrice wandered outside to the garden, breathing in the crisp fresh air. Patrice had her fill of champagne, the bubbles rising headily and pleasantly through her body, and she felt emboldened to test James' true feelings for her. She willed that James would follow her outside so that she could finally confront him with her feelings. If the man was going to be so damned stubborn, she would have to push him along, gently helping him bend to her.

Patrice knew he held some regard for her, for why else was James riveted to her every movement? In any case, it was time to prove that theory once and for all. Patrice hummed a tune under her breath to calm her beating heart as she strolled through the lush garden. Small torches lit the path for those who would make their way outside for a brief interlude or a moment of solitude. As expected, moments later, she heard footsteps on the gravel. She knew without looking that it was James. She felt him in every cell of her body.

"You are very foolish to come alone to the gardens," James whispered as he approached.

Patrice faced him confidently. "I knew you would come, and so you have. I am so very glad you came."

James lifted his hands to her elbows and then shifted them down to her small waist, pulling her tightly to his chest. Patrice trembled as she whispered against his lips, "Kiss me, you stubborn man."

She leaned into James, wrapping her arms tightly around his neck. He was so close, and she could feel the way his restraint left him trembling, his will alone keeping him from ravishing her. It wasn't until Patrice took the first step, her lips brushing as softly as a feather across his, that she felt the dam burst within them both. Their kiss exploded into a frenzied longing that neither could have imagined. James' breathing quickened, his lips hot against her flushed skin, as he kissed Patrice's neck and ears, his hands sweeping up from her waist to cup the beautiful mounds of her bosom. He was ravenous, and Patrice's gentle attempt to match him aroused him more than any experienced courtesan had ever done. She was a beckoning angel, and he was ensnared by her, body and soul.

Sanity returned to him briefly when he realized that he had pushed her against a garden wall, the rough stone scraping the fabric of her dress. He grabbed her hands, pulling them from where they were tangled in his hair, and spoke in a tormented whisper, "Patrice, we cannot continue like this. Someone could discover us."

Patrice wrested her hands free and grabbed his waistcoat, pulling him against her with unexpected force. "I don't care anymore, James. I don't care about anything but being with you. I long for you. I ache for you. Please, James." With that she kissed him gently, sliding her fingers back into his hair and sending chills racing down his body.

James groaned, "Patrice, what have you done to me?"

"Nothing that you have not also done to me. I want you, James." She kissed him deeply and as she did so, she slid one hand down his body to grip his hardness. She gasped at the girth she felt there but stroked eagerly as James bucked in her hands, a low growl escaping his lips. She kissed his neck and ears as he rubbed himself in her palm, only stopping when he felt release dangerously close. James broke their kiss and spun Patrice so her back was to him, and her front pressed against the stone wall. She gasped as he swept her hair from the back of her neck, trailing kisses along her shoulders. Desperately, he reached around her and grasped for the hem of her dress, pulling up what felt like yards of fabric until at last he felt the satin-softness of her thighs. He didn't wait, nor did he warn her, but instead plunged his hand between her legs to the silken warmth he knew waited there.

Patrice cried out when he began stroking the delicate bundle of nerves at her apex, and he quickly covered her mouth with his free hand, stroking in vigorous circles as her wetness enveloped his fingers.

Patrice felt on fire, surely, she was burning, as the rough scrape of his fingers against her ignited a need she'd never known. She was lost, utterly at his mercy, her entire being focused only on the heat of each sweep of his fingers. Her legs trembled and she moaned against his hand which still covered his mouth.

"This is insanity," James whispered, his voice husky against the back of her neck. But, oh, she would be undone by this man and his fingers which continued their torturous circles between her legs.

"I know that there is more to lovemaking than this," she gasped. James dropped his hand from her mouth but did not stop his fingers between her legs. She felt the heat building in her, reaching for some pinnacle she'd never seen before. "I will not stop until I have had my fill of you, James."

Patrice couldn't believe that the wanton voice she heard was her own. James dropped his hands from her skirts then, and pulled her further into the darkness, holding her hand as he led the way into the deepest part of the garden until he found a place he thought would be safe for their dangerous game.

"This is insanity," James repeated, hearing his voice as if from a distance. Any semblance of the reality that he found himself in seemed unreal. Only this moment, and this woman who belonged to him, mattered and was real and true. James lifted Patrice to sit up on the ledge of a small stone wall and stepped between her legs to kiss her again.

Patrice put her fingers to his lips and whispered, "It's not insanity, James. It was insane that you waited this long to come to me." James kissed Patrice's fingertips as she tried to wrap her legs around him but was frustrated in her attempts by her skirts.

James groaned and he swept her skirts up finding precisely what he was looking for, the opening of her fine silk drawers. Patrice's head fell back as James again brushed her delicate cleft with his strong fingers. As she whimpered in ecstasy, James made a visceral growl and lowered his head to her thighs where he replaced what his fingers had done earlier with deft sweeps of his tongue. Patrice let her head fall back, soft sighs escaping with each flick of her apex. James was a man consumed. He wanted nothing more than to lose himself with Patrice, *in* Patrice, for as long as he could. His entire existence felt boiled down to eliciting each moan from her lips, each flex of her thighs on either side of his head. It took all his power to keep his focus on the slick velvet of this woman. At last, with one last playful caress of his tongue, he felt Patrice tense against his lips, shuddering and panting, as her delicious orgasm filled his mouth.

When he rose again to look upon her, their souls seemed to touch when they met each other's eyes. Patrice's eyes, he noticed, brimmed with crystalline tears.

"Why do you cry, my love?" James asked as he gently swept the tears from her cheeks.

"James," Patrice murmured, "this is a dream. A wonderful dream I hoped and prayed would come true: that you would be here in my arms, forever."

At this James paused, his sanity returning slowly. Honor demanded that he be truthful with Patrice and that she harbor no girlish fantasies where he was concerned. James had to be transparent.

"Patrice, I cannot marry you. That is why I stayed away from you. This is torture for us both, and this could ruin you for any other proper marriage. I care for you too much to allow that to happen."

Patrice felt an iciness run through her body. He would deny them love, even now. She pushed him away and smoothed her skirts. "James, why on earth do you refuse what is right in front of you? I have professed my feelings in no uncertain terms. Could it be that you are incapable of love? Or is it just *me* you can never love?"

"No Patrice, you have nothing to do with my views on matrimony. You must believe me." James remained stoic as Patrice raised his hands to her mouth and gently kissed them. She looked into his eyes.

"James, I would never hurt you."

James sighed and stepped back, holding Patrice's arms at length. "I know that you are unlike any woman I have ever known," he said, "And you are nothing like the woman who raised me, who dared to call herself my mother. Patrice, I know you are good and true, but I closed my heart to the idea of marriage, and I will never open it again. Not even for you. All I can give you are brief moments, and you deserve more. You deserve a husband and children."

Patrice moved away from James, her eyes brimming with unshed tears of anguish.

"Patrice," James pleaded, "you once called me a coward, and perhaps I am. I cannot trust myself to love you as you should be loved."

Patrice tried to compose herself as best she could. She saw the pain in her lover's eyes, but she was immune to it, cold even, while her pain consumed her so deeply.

"I had hoped you would finally see the truth that lay between us. But I was wrong." Patrice choked back tears, bitterness in her tone. "You will never put the past behind you, even as a happy future and a home filled with love lay before you, beckoning you to just… reach for it…But no, you will not. You prefer to hang on to…what is it, James? Hate and bitterness? So, it seems you were right all along. I cannot be with you. I will go. I will live my life, fully and completely. I will one day have children of my own, a home, and a husband whom I will love and honor."

James' eyes lit with hurt, but Patrice continued. "But you…you will live the rest of your life as a bitter, lonely man. I wish to God I would never have to see you again." Patrice started back towards the manse.

"Patrice, wait, please," James called after her. He stepped toward her, reaching for her, when without warning, the whole world went up in flames.

James called to Patrice as she ran down the garden path back to the main house. He heard the explosion before his mind could process its terrible aftermath. It seemed to originate from one of the closed terraces on the main floor of the dining hall and was immediately followed by a reverberation that shook the very ground he stood on.

Patrice was closest to the terrace when the explosion occurred, the force of the blast throwing her at least ten feet off the garden path. It was as if everything had gone underwater and into the slowest motion. She felt a scorching blast of air that swept her feet off the ground, tossing her into the shrubbery of the garden. Before Patrice's mind shut down, she heard James' anguished cry. Her soft lips curled into a faint smile as she drifted off into the velvet blackness.

James reached Patrice, scanning her in search of broken bones. James prayed that in moving her he would not somehow worsen her condition, but he knew he had best get her back and attended to by a doctor. James gathered Patrice in his arms, carrying her to the veranda where the assemblage gathered to escape the flames and smoke from within.

"Is there a doctor? This woman needs help!" James called, as he moved through the crowd.

"James? Patrice!" Patrice's mother, Angelica, ran forward, placing her hands on her daughter's face and smoothing the hair away from her brow. Angelica choked back tears, but looked at James and asked, "What happened?"

"She was coming back from the gardens," James stammered, "We must find a place to lay her down to rest." James pushed through to the edge of the veranda until he found an unoccupied spot. "There are blankets from the guest house. She needs to be kept warm." James entreated Patrice's worried mother.

James removed his coat and covered Patrice as her father joined them, worry etched across his features.

"Rittenhouse, how did this happen?" Corchoran asked with great concern.

"Sir, your daughter was hurt by the blast from within the house. Thankfully, she was far enough away from the house that no debris hit her."

Tom Corchoran searched James's face, noting the dark

furrows that framed his visage and showed deep in his eyes. He placed his hand on James' shoulder. "Thank you, son, for rescuing Patrice as you did."

James was ashamed of this show of gratitude by Patrice's father when in truth he had behaved the scoundrel just moments before the accident. Were it not for his short-sighted passions, Patrice would never have remained outside so long and might have escaped any harm to her person. Now, James had to worry that along with her broken heart, her body might be hurt as well, all thanks to him. He raked a hand through his hair.

Corchoran, spoke again, shaking James free from his thoughts. "James, you must go and help Gregory contain the fire." This seemed to rouse James.

James shook his head. "I cannot leave Patrice."

Just then an esteemed doctor from the Royal household who had been attending the festivities found them. "Lord Rittenhouse, Mr. Corchoran, please step away so that I can assess the young woman."

The doctor felt for broken bones and checked her scalp for any cuts or contusions. He pressed his ear to Patrice's chest and listened to her heartbeat and breathing. Finally, he leaned back and sighed. "Good," he said, looking up at the two men. "She has suffered no breaks in her bones, and her scalp seems unaffected. Her breathing is steady and strong. I think she will be fine."

He leaned back up and smiled reassuringly. Angelica had just returned with blankets and heard these last words from the good doctor, tears coursing down her cheeks in relief. She rushed to cover her daughter in blankets.

Tom Corchoran put his hand on James' shoulder. "Go now where you are most needed; we will be fine here. Gregory has been seeking your help inside."

James was in a trance of self-condemnation. Corchoran more insistently roused him again. "James," Corchoran spoke firmly, placing a hand on James's shoulder. He looked at Corchoran with questioning eyes.

"My wife and I will tend to Patrice. She will be fine." Corchoran said this with forced confidence. James nodded and reluctantly stood and moved inside towards the fire.

Only moments before, smoke began billowing from the dining hall, through the foyer, making its way toward the ballroom. Gregory was quickly alerted by one of his staff that it appeared a fire may have started in the dining hall. Gregory searched for James but to no avail. Luckily, his eyes found his father-in-law, Jacques.

"Jacques, I need some assistance. Ladies, will you excuse us?" Without waiting for an answer, Gregory led a surprised Jacques away from his wife and friends. Once Gregory found a quiet spot he whispered urgently. "Please alert the assembly to exit the ballroom to the veranda as a precautionary measure. It seems we have a fire."

Jacques was surprised, but nodded and quickly made

his way to the center of the ballroom where he made his announcement to the surprised guests. In the meantime, Gregory made haste to the dining hall through the foyer where indeed billows of smoke wafted from the kitchen and dining halls. Gregory was filled with dread as he realized that flames accompanied the billowing smoke. He shouted to several of his dutiful staff who joined the male guests of the party, all of whom immediately came to assist. It was then that he heard the explosion that came from the dining hall's terrace.

"Quickly, we need to arrange a bucket brigade!" Gregory shouted. "Our hand pump is out in the back. We need a minimum of forty men to make our brigade standing arms length." Gregory turned to his man. "Grab all the buckets with your staff and go. Make haste, man!"

Off they all ran. Gregory turned to the remaining men who stood with him. "Now for the rest of us, let's pull the drapes down as quickly as we can. Hurry!"

Just then, Gregory glimpsed his wife through the thickening smoke. His blood was already racing through his veins with fear and now anger made it surge into his heart.

"What in the hell are you doing here? Get back, Gabrielle."

"I wish to help — I can be a part of the brigade just as any of you men!" Gabrielle's tone was firm and insistent.

Gregory stormed over to her, grabbing her by her shoulders. "This is not the time for disobedience. Get back to the patio or I swear I will carry you there myself!"

Gabrielle had never seen her husband as angry as he was at that moment. Her fear for all their lives kept her temper in check and she hastened out the back to the veranda, angry and frightened. "Damn the man," Gabrielle thought. "I can and will protect my home and my husband."

Gabrielle rushed to the servants who were doling out buckets, getting in line and shouting out orders to the surprise of the men around her. Gregory worked alongside the men closest to the flames, methodically focused completely on tossing bucket after bucket of water onto the inferno.

Henry, Gregory's man, appeared at his shoulder suddenly, saying in a frustrated voice, "Milord, your lady is indeed outside, however, she is part of the brigade and will not leave the line."

She was outrageous. He grit his teeth in frustration. There would be time enough for her later after they'd saved his home. Gregory called out to the men who were far down the line. "Keep the pumps going! And fill the buckets to the rim!"

Suddenly, James was at Gregory's side. Gregory redoubled his efforts, sweat streaming down his brow and his back and James quickly settled into a rhythm, grabbing buckets to throw on the fire and doubling their pace.

After several hours, together they were able to control the fire and keep it from spreading to any other areas of the home. When at last they could breathe, Gregory turned to thank his friend, only to pause at the worried look in his friend's eyes. "James, the worst is now over. All we need to do now is manage the few embers that remain. If you are needed elsewhere…"

Reluctantly, James informed Gregory of Patrice's injury, adding, "Gregory, I may be the last person she wants to see when she opens her eyes." Nevertheless, he took his friend's advice and went back out to check on Patrice.

Gabrielle refused to leave the site all through the night. She held her place on the fire brigade until her arms were numb. She would not abandon her husband or her home. She battled on through the smoke, the fatigue and the numbness. Did Gregory not yet understand her character?

Just then Gabrielle saw her husband. He'd long ago shed his coat and his white dress shirt was open, covered in soot and grime. His face was tired as he ran a hand through his thick hair, searching for her. Even in all his exhaustion, he was the most beautiful man Gabrielle had ever seen. She held her breath as their eyes found one another and Gregory rushed over, moving every obstacle out of his way until he was before her. Gabrielle cried out as Gregory embraced her passionately, kissing her as if they were the only two people in the world.

When Gabrielle finally released Gregory from her

embrace, she noted the sadness in his eyes. "What is it?" she asked.

"Come, you need to see to Patrice. She was hurt in the blast, but do not worry she is tended to now.".

"Oh no! Where is she?" Gabrielle grabbed her dirtied skirts and immediately went in search of her friend, her husband trailing after her.

Gregory held his wife's hand tightly as they moved through the remaining clusters of guests until they found Patrice, tended to by her parents and James Rittenhouse. Patrice's eyes were open, and she exclaimed when she saw her friend.

"Gabrielle!" Patrice smiled with relief. "I heard you were aiding in the bucket brigade! Lord Stalward would you ever have guessed that your wife would be such a helpmate in the most difficult of times?"

Gregory ran the palm of his hand against his wife's supple back, sending shivers down her spine that had nothing to do with the cold night air. Gregory answered Patrice all the while looking deeply into his wife's stormy blue eyes. "Patrice, I am forever surprised by my wife. Although I will never allow her to risk her life like this again under any circumstance." Gregory smiled to take the heat out of his words. Gabrielle said nothing as she knelt by her friend's side. Gregory and James nodded to one another, relieved that all were well.

"What on earth happened to you?" Gabrielle asked.

Patrice took a deep breath, avoiding James' gaze. "I

decided to take a turn in the garden to clear my head from the champagne when suddenly there was a blast that threw me to the ground. Thankfully, I was found safely and brought here to recover. I am fine, Gabrielle. Completely fine," Patrice assured her friend.

"So, who is this mystery savior of yours?" Gabrielle asked with a sly smile, and then more quietly so only Patrice could hear her, "As if I have to ask."

Patrice looked up, the color rising in her cheeks. Gabrielle raised her brow. When no one replied to her inquiry Gabrielle continued, "Well, so long as you were rescued unharmed, the rest of it makes no difference."

Patrice laid her head on her mother's shoulder and closed her eyes as Gabrielle held her hand, worried more for Patrice's heart than any risk to her body.

Hours later, the last of the guests had been safely escorted back to their homes as the immediate family, friends, and staff staying at the Montrose Estate slowly made their way to their private quarters. Luckily, the fire was contained to the kitchen and dining hall on the first floor. Below the first floor where the staff maintained their expansive residence, all was safely persevered having experienced no smoke or water damage.

Patrice, leaning gratefully against her father and Gregory, was escorted to her room. She had refused James' help, much to his consternation. Patrice remembered all too well the events that led up to her accident and her heart bristled at the memory of James' rejection. Patrice longed for her bed so she could escape her painful thoughts with sleep.

Finally, alone in her chambers and satisfied that all staying at Montrose Estate were safe, Gabrielle had washed and wrapped herself in one of Gregory's warm robes as hers was too flimsy for what her body craved. Coming off the panic and rush of the firefighting, Gabrielle felt unexpectedly chilled and so carefully lit her fireplace and candles. She sat in an armchair close to the hearth and watched the flames dance, amazed at how fire could bring such comfort after the fear and pain it had brought these last hours. Gabrielle shivered in her exhaustion and relief. She poured a brandy as her thoughts turned to her husband.

She had been incensed by her husband's stubbornness in refusing her help. Many of their guests attending the ball had foolishly cowered on the veranda instead of helping, and even fewer women assisted. Gabrielle gripped her brandy glass, vowing bitterly that she would never be placed in a corner of impotence in any situation, especially one where the lives of her loved ones were in such peril. It was time she and her husband had it out on this matter. She took a sip of her brandy to bolster her courage, knowing the battle she faced against her imposing husband. Still, unbidden images of Gregory leading the group in putting out the fire, the sweat and grime on his strong brow, his muscles bulging through the damp shirt mingled with Gabrielle's anger, turning to a physical longing.

It was just then that Gregory swept the door open, shutting it swiftly behind him, and leaned against it, eyes closed. Gabrielle, her body suddenly on fire, rose to greet him, letting the dressing gown fall open as she pressed herself against his length, her naked flesh clinging to him.

"Gregory," she whispered urgently as she kissed his neck.

Gregory groaned loudly, taking her wrists in his hands and pulling them overhead. In one deft movement, he flipped their positions and pressed her back to the door, wrists pinned. as he turned her back to the door. "What is it Gabrielle? The excitement of tonight has made you long for me? Does disobeying my wishes make you hot for me?"

Gabrielle did not like the tone in his voice, despite the truth of his words. She'd felt a thrill tonight, fighting the fire alongside her husband and the bucket brigade, a power flooding her body that she did as she pleased for herself and for those she loved. She was about to say the same when Gregory banished all thoughts from her mind. Her head fell backward as he roughly cupped her right breast, squeezing her already taut nipples to the point of pain. She cried out at the sharpness of it, though she felt the slickness and heat intensify between her legs.

Gregory then abruptly pulled away, panting heavily. "Yes, you are a wild thing. You have always been wild, and you always will be, and you will never listen to me, will you?" Gregory pushed away from her in frustration as he swept his dark hair off his brow. Gabrielle reached for him, surprised by the fire and despair written across his features.

"Gregory," Gabrielle panted, "I do listen to you. I honor you as my husband and my lover. But tonight we had to work together. I am your wife. I am not an ornament that merely decorates your home. I will always work by your side or what else is the point of being married? Gregory, I need you now, please." Gabrielle shrugged her husband's robe off her shoulders, her long golden hair glistening in the firelight, cascaded down her lithe back, as she wrapped her arms around him.

"I could have lost you tonight," Gregory murmured, tracing the lines of her arms around his neck. When he looked into her eyes, he saw tears brimming atop her gorgeous lashes. At last, he understood her need to be his partner, his equal, and that in the face of danger, her bravery would keep her with him. She too realized that all of Gregory's harsh words, his seemingly restrictive wishes, boiled down to one inexorable fact: he was terrified of losing her.

"Oh Gregory," she whispered, tightening her hold around him. Gregory was undone. Gabrielle sensed his surrender as her hands raced across his skin, ripping tattered and worn garments off his back. Gregory gathered her hair in his hands at her back as he caressed her buttocks.

Gabrielle pressed the length of her body against him,

relishing the press of her breasts against his bare chest. They were consumed, mindless, and lost to their lust. He took a step back, but before he could unfasten his trousers, her fingers were already there, ripping the laces and yanking the fabric off his slender hips. When at last his massive manhood sprang free, Gabrielle knelt before him, grasping his hips in her hands and took the full length of his shaft into her mouth. Gregory groaned, legs trembling. When she began working him, her tongue teasing up and down his length, he slammed a hand into the door to steady himself.

She took him deep until he hit the back of her throat before sliding back and teasing his tip gently with her tongue and teeth. Gregory was enslaved by her just as she was by him. Their shared passion, and lust for one another was magnetic, and the events from the evening only made their desire and need that much more primal. With his free hand, he grabbed a fistful of her hair, holding her head gently as she continued to hold him captive. Slowly, he began thrusting himself in and out of her waiting mouth, letting her tongue tease every inch of him. He picked up speed, careful to give Gabrielle time to breathe around him, but she took him every time, groaning so that he felt the vibrations down his shaft. Her fingernails dug into the flesh at his hips, driving him faster still until he felt certain he would explode, spilling himself down her throat.

When he was nearly at his precipice, Gregory pulled himself from her mouth, the full length of him gleaming, swollen, and ready to burst. He grasped Gabrielle by her shoulders and yanked her to her feet, lifting her in one solid movement so she could wrap her long legs around his waist. Neither of them cared to wait any longer. Gregory buried himself deep within Gabrielle's soaking wet center, pressing her back against the door and cradling her buttocks in his hands.

"Yes," Gabrielle whispered. She worked her hips and Gregory plunged in and out with such force the door rattled in its frame. Claiming her mouth in a deep kiss, the two were lost in each other, moans echoing in their bodies. Against the hard plane of the door, Gregory pumped hard into Gabrielle with such ferocity that in moments, he felt her inner muscles tighten around him. Her nails dug into his shoulders as her first release tore through her, ripping a feral scream from her mouth. When she relaxed again, draped across his shoulders, Gregory carried her to their bed, sucking and licking her breasts along the way. All the while, Gabrielle clung to her husband's shoulders longing to kiss every muscle of Gregory's hard body.

Gregory gently laid her down on the edge of their bed all the while dipping his head to kiss Gabrielle's body as she in turn caressed and delighted in the feel of his long hard body and shoulders, groaning even more as her body soared in painful ecstasy. He stood above her, smiling at his wife's lustful abandon, and pulled out of her as he reached between her legs to rub the sensitive nub between her legs. He wanted to watch her again; he relished how her body writhed and swayed, sweat beading across her skin, eyes closed and fingers gripping the sheets. He rubbed faster, tracing circles with his fingers as he slipped his thumb down further to slide into her opening. Gabrielle moaned, her thighs quaking, and Gregory knew she was getting close. Her breasts swayed, her nipples hard and peaked. Gregory relished all that he could do, all that he could make her feel. At last, when Gabrielle's breaths came in little, frantic whimpers, Gregory removed his hand and entered her in one smooth thrust. Gabrielle's head slammed back into the mattress, her back bowing, as she immediately climaxed.

"Gregory, I love you. I love you. Don't ever let me go," she panted. At those words, Gregory's mind snapped as he looked down at his wild bride and grabbed her face between his hands.

"Say that again." Gregory's look was fierce as Gabrielle hesitated. He gently shook her. "Say that again."

Gabrielle's eyes filled with tears that spilled over her lashes as she looked deeply into his own. "I love you, Gregory. I love you."

Gregory groaned as he kissed her gently, his tongue between her lips as he continued his thrusts. He moved his fingers between them and softly rubbed her nub and her body began to shudder again in climax. With his one free hand, he grabbed her breast, flicking her nipple in time with his thrusts as his fingers softly moved between them at her apex with his other hand. Gabrielle shuddered once...

twice…and then her orgasm overtook her with such strength she saw stars. Gregory joined her with his own long, thundering release.

Many hours later, as the sun slowly crept into their warm bedchamber, the exhausted couple, comfortably and safely wrapped in each other's arms and legs, smiled blissfully before closing their eyes in sweet sleep.

Gregory kissed Gabrielle's forehead speaking softly. "And I love you, my wife. I have always loved you."

Gabrielle smiled, her sleepy eyes now closed, and sighed as she snuggled into her husband's arms, a single tear escaping down her warm cheek.

FAILED EXPECTATIONS

The Ton was a-twitter with tales of the bravery and courage shown by the handsome Duke's Lord Staward and Rittenhouse. The women swooned in the retelling of the heroism the men showed when they led the effort to douse the flames at the Montrose Estate. Always searching for new heroes and villains, the Ton suggested that the fire was likely an act of arson by someone jealous of the great Lord Stalward and his beautiful duchess.

The only person who was not thrilled at the success and heroism at Montrose Estate was Lord Norwood. Indeed, the night of the fire, Norwood had not slept. He sat in his drawing room sipping from a nearly empty bottle of whiskey as he bitterly recalled the events of the evening. He had paid his man in gold coins to ensure the burning of the estate, and instead, his plan petered out in the same way the flames did under Stalward's watch.

"Damn the man!" Norwood exclaimed, slamming his whiskey glass onto the arm of his chair. Norwood had suffered years of embarrassment at the hands of the Martins and now Lord Stalward, and all in society were well aware that Norwood had been shut out of the waterworks project. How he hated these people. He longed to finally find himself triumphant over these ingrates and thought that the fire would be his way to finally exact his revenge.

Instead, Stalward became the Ton's latest hero in his deft handling of the fire at his home. What was it with these people that they were able to always circumvent any of his machinations? Norwood seethed as he threw back the last of the whiskey and cleared his throat. His henchman Alf entered his study, tentatively, with his hat tucked in his beefy hands.

"Come in and close the door behind you," Norwood barked. Alf scuttled sheepishly into the office. "You are a damned fool! How could you fail me so miserably? I will have you return every penny to me you giant oaf. Only winners get paid!" Norwood exclaimed. He leaped from his chair, the whiskey having affected his balance more than he realized.

Norwood thought he'd planned the details perfectly and he had Alf, a brute from the jails in Scotland, execute everything for the inferno. All was set forth as planned and no one suspected that this had been an act of arson. The blaze had been somewhat successful, having hurt several ball attendees, and inflicted cosmetic damage to the

Stalward's home. But not a hair had been harmed on the heads of those Norwood most coveted.

"Sir, your wife let me in so you may wish to lower your voice," Alf responded with eerie calm. He had long ago learned how to soothe his savage master.

"Do you think I care about that insipid bitch? She knows her place," Norwood sneered. He stood inches from Alf's face, spittle forming into a frothing foam at the corners of his mouth. "You failed me. Now that bastard Stalward will be ever more vigilant, and I will never have the same opportunity to destroy him again! *You are an incompetent fool!*"

Improbably, Alf lowered his eyes in submission despite being a full foot taller than Norwood. "Your grace, I know that tonight did not come off as planned but you can still have your vengeance."

"And how do you propose we do that? They will be on high alert, and I will never succeed in destroying them." Norwood groaned as he took another drink.

"Pardon me, Milord, but there is a way to destroy them. To do so will leave them with no honor and gut them to their core. My plan is a far crueler way to achieve your revenge." Norwood looked up at the giant and waited for him to continue.

"We know that Martin's daughter, Gabrielle, is a great horsewoman. Well, I learned from one of the Stalward's maids that she rides every day....and alone."

"What?" Norwood asked his henchman incredulously.

Alf responded calmly and slowly "She rides alone… apparently, she even rides in plain shirt and britches."

"She is a heathen, just like her mother," Norwood huffed. "But what of it? How can this help us in any way?"

Alf cleared his throat as he continued, "Well Milord a young woman galloping around the countryside is bound to attract the worst sort of men. Anything could happen…"

"Perhaps you're right, but after last night's fire, they will be vigilant," Norwood replied, unconvinced.

Alf took a small step forward as he persisted in laying out his plan. "Milord, her maid says that she runs her horses almost every day. She will return to riding soon enough. And when she does, we will be waiting for her, and you will have your revenge once and for all. The duke is said to be very attached to his young wife. And she is Martin's only daughter."

Norwood reluctantly saw the truth in this and grimaced. "This is your last chance Alf, and this time I will make sure that the deed is done myself." Norwood smiled thinking about the terrified, desperate look on the duke's wife's face, how she would beg and plead with him to have mercy. Just then a sound from outside the door startled Norwood from his daydream. Norwood swung the door open and looked both ways, but no one was in the quiet foyer.

Norwood closed the door firmly behind him, after casting one last long glance around the quiet foyer and resumed his planning with Alf. As Norwood closed the door behind him, neither one of the men was the wiser as his timid wife, Clara, moved quietly from behind the large clock in the foyer, and raced up the stairs to her bedroom.

UNSETTLED LOVERS

*E*ight days after the ball and the terrible fire, Gabrielle awoke to find her husband still asleep in bed next to her. "Thank goodness," she thought and smiled as she kissed his forehead. Gregory, James, and her father had spent the last week in a fervor of handling the fire's aftermath, setting the builders to restore what had been damaged.

The men were all convinced that the fire was the result of some foul play. Although no one knew for certain who the culprit might be, Gregory had his suspicions. Norwood had a motive and knew his property well. As farfetched as the idea of him seeking this sort of retribution, Gregory could not put it past the man. Gregory recalled how Norwood had smirked at him all evening long at the ball as if he held some secret. Gregory's intuition told him that Norwood was somehow responsible, but he could not speak of this out loud, especially in front of Gabrielle and Patrice. Patrice and her parents, along with Gabrielle, would be deeply troubled that Patrice's beloved and woe-begotten Aunt Clara could be in the presence of, and perhaps victimized by such treachery. Gregory decided to keep his suspicions to himself until he could learn more from the detectives he hired.

After the fire, Gregory had ordered that all the men fan out with lanterns around the property looking for some clue as to what might have caused the fire. James had ridden far to the south of the Montrose estate when he spied the first set of tracks on a dirt road leading to the rear of the property. They were carriage marks of some sort, and the etchings of the wheels on the road looked to be from a finer carriage, as their wheels were sometimes etched with engravings of grapes and fern, which could easily be discerned in one mud patch. James took note of its details and headed back to the estate to join his friends. They would set out the next day together to look at the tracks and see if there was anything that could give them any further clues that could identify the culprits.

The families that had surrounded the Stalwards at the Montrose Estate in joyful preparation, remained in the aftermath of the fire to offer the young couple, as well as themselves comfort. On the evening of the ninth day, most of the families decided they would depart after dinner. The cooks prepared a wonderful meal of venison and dumplings followed by blackberry pie. The group settled into a lighter banter than they had allowed themselves for several days. It was only after the men had sojourned for their cigars and cognac that the discussion arose again about finding the culprit in what each of them believed had been an act of arson.

When the married men took their leave that evening, clearly seeking the sanctuary and warmth of their women, James remained alone downstairs and decided he would take his whiskey out to the gardens. There he reminisced about his evening with Patrice that had ended so disastrously. He wished he could feel some remorse for his actions but could only relish in the memory of holding her in his arms, tasting her seductive kisses, and feeling the slick heat that flowed between her legs after just a touch from him. Patrice bewitched him like no other woman ever had. And now seeing her every day here knowing she was in the same home as he, was more than a little torture to his body and his heart.

James recalled the explosion, and his body tensed as he relived his fear when he saw his beautiful siren lifted off her feet by the force of the blast. In that moment, the pain he felt at having left her so harshly was something for which he would never forgive himself. Thank God she had survived the blast unscathed, but the trauma ignited something in his soul that felt like a similar longing he had experienced when he was but a young boy wishing for a caring mother. James felt trapped, wanting her and yet so afraid to love. Finally, James found himself back at the manse. He stood outside, looking up at the impressive façade for several moments, before he decided he was tired enough to retire for the night. It was then that he saw her. Patrice was sitting at the edge of the veranda wearing her drawing robe and slippers.

James cleared his throat to alert her she was not alone. "You shouldn't be out here by yourself. Your hosts would be very upset with you, as would your parents."

Patrice looked over her shoulder but stubbornly refused to acknowledge a word he had spoken. James sighed and walked to where she sat, knowing he could not leave her there alone. "Miss Corchoran, you must now allow me to escort you back inside."

"I do not care a whit about what you think, *James,*" Patrice sounded out his name sarcastically, clearly mocking the absurdity of his using her formal name when they were alone, after all that had passed between them.

"Patrice," he tried again, "you cannot stay out here alone, and I am too exhausted to argue with you. Let's return inside."

"No. You are certainly no protector, as well I know after recent incidents." She stood glaring at him. "I will return when I am good and ready."

"Patrice, I understand your feelings towards me, but you must return into the house, and promise to never wander outside alone again. These are dangerous times. Now please let's go back in."

Patrice knew that his words were rational, but she didn't care. "No," she said simply.

James laughed at this. "Patrice, you are being ridiculous."

But Patrice was defiant. "I will never listen to anything you have to say, James Rittenhouse. You mean nothing to me."

On hearing those words from Patrice's lips, something snapped in James' heart, and he reached for her hand, his breath mingling with hers. He grasped her shoulders. She dared to smile mockingly up at him.

"Do you hear me, James?" she whispered, her bitterness spilling forth relentlessly, "You mean nothing to me! I am going to marry well, and I will be devoted to my husband, and have his babies. I won't even remember who you are!" There was venom in her words, though a tear escaped her eye, which proved to be James' undoing.

He sighed and held her close. "What am I going to do with you, woman?" Patrice, angry at her tears pushed against him. He groaned and Patrice abruptly stopped moving, sensing intuitively that her movements created an intimacy that she did not want to tempt herself with.

"Fine, you win. I want to go back in. James, let me go," Patrice tried once again to wrest herself away from James. It took all his willpower, once again, to let Patrice go. But he knew he would be playing with both their hearts if he held her for one moment longer. He released her, running a hand through his hair in obvious frustration.

Patrice ran swiftly back into the house.

James watched her leave and his heart swelled with pain, longing, regret....and, dare he think it, love... He loved this woman. He needed this woman, and she wanted him. James slowly returned to the house, making sure he locked the doors carefully behind him. He knew he would have a sleepless night ahead.

AN UNWANTED DETOUR

The next morning, just as the inky night sky faded to sunrise, Gabrielle carefully slipped out of bed, tiptoeing to her wardrobe where she retrieved her riding britches, shirt, and vest. She made her way to the door, glancing over her shoulder at her sleeping husband. Once out the door, Gabrielle leaped down the stairs, grabbed her boots and crop, and made way for the stables. She and Patrice had planned to meet early this morning and ride to the beaches of Ramsgate and back before anyone could stop them.

Patrice was already waiting, fully dressed, and tending to her stallion. She smiled when she saw Gabrielle sprinting towards her. "Good morning! Slow down, Gabrielle. What is the rush?" Patrice asked with a smile. Gabrielle ignored her friend and continued running to the stable, and quickly readied her horse.

"Gabrielle, what is the matter? Please do not tell me that Gregory is unaware of our plans for the day?" Patrice asked again, this time with a hint of chastisement in her voice.

Gabrielle laughed nervously. "My husband is mercifully still abed, and when he awakens, which could be any second…well, no he will not be pleased to learn of our plans to ride to the beaches today. He was overprotective even before the fire. Gregory prefers to have me, er, close at hand."

Gabrielle recalled the wondrous evening she shared with her husband and smiled, thinking about her handsome lord's broad shoulders above her as she spent herself in unfettered joy beneath him just a few hours ago.

Gabrielle shook herself back to reality, looking back at Patrice. She thought she noticed dark circles under her friend's eyes. "Are you feeling all right Patrice? You look tired and stressed. Please tell me if you still feel up to a ride this morning—we can cancel if you prefer."

"Oh no! I am perfectly fine! The sea air will do me good. And I long to leave the grounds today," Patrice said wistfully, turning away as Gabrielle approached her, probing softly.

"Patrice, I saw you with James Rittenhouse last night out on the veranda, from my bedroom window. I just went to close it—and I saw you both. You two seemed deep in… conversation. Is everything all right Patrice?"

Patrice responded with a slight shrug of her shoulders. This prompted Gabrielle to blurt out something she had wished to say for weeks to her dearest friend. "Patrice, please forgive my interference but I honestly believe the man adores you. I have secretly hoped that he would admit his feelings for you."

Patrice took a sharp breath pulling herself up as best she could, turning her back as she prepared her horse for the ride. Gabrielle touched her friend's arm gently. "Patrice, please don't be angry with me, I know that there is something between you two."

Patrice did not trust herself to speak of James and keep her composure, and she knew that any lie would immediately be seen for what it was by Gabrielle. "Gabrielle," Patrice spoke finally at last, "can we pretend just for the day that we are the young girls from last summer with not a care in the world? Please."

Gabrielle hesitated and then smiled, taking Patrice's hands into her own. "My dear, yes, today we will forget all things except enjoying each other's company, and the beautiful sea awaiting us." Gabrielle hugged Patrice quickly and walked towards her horse.

"Now do let's hurry as the day is getting ahead of us!" Patrice spoke brightly to abate the sadness in her heavy heart. Grabbing the reins, she managed to arrange herself sidesaddle. Patrice smiled as she watched her less conventional friend jump fully astride onto her own stallion's back. "I wonder if Lord Gregory approves of his wife riding about Ramsgate in her bloomers!" Patrice laughed teasing Gabrielle.

"Ha! Maybe not. However, Lord Gregory has learned to accept the peccadillos of his wife." Gabrielle smiled, throwing her head back. "Let's see if you can keep up!"

Norwood lay in wait at the edge of the forest abutting the Montrose estate, with two of his men, including Alf, waiting to catch sight of his prize. Alf learned from Gabrielle's maidservant that she had planned to meet Patrice that morning for a ride to Ramsgate's beaches. This was the opportunity Norwood had longed for to finally and definitively punish the men who had dared impugn his reputation and refuse him any access to the London waterworks project. That Norwood would be denied its rightful place in history because of these peons galled him to no end. Not even his father-in-law, the Earl could affect this turn of events.

Norwood's disappointment was great as he had watched his plan for setting the Montrose House on fire had not succeeded in destroying his enemies. Norwood could not fathom that his adversaries would be able to overcome his well-planned machinations. But he was a patient man, one who always played the odds to his benefit. He had worked through the second pathway he had chosen to deal with Gregory and Jacques, and this time his plan would work.

This time he would personally make sure that all would be accomplished as he had envisioned.

Norwood spotted the women on horseback heading towards the beaches of Ramsgate. His breath remained steady, despite his quickening excitement as he spied his niece Patrice riding sidesaddle behind his primary target, Gabrielle, who wore her men's britches and riding coat. Patrice would be a casualty of his revenge, but Norwood found that he was pleased by the prospect of striking fear into her heart, too, such was his hatred for Stalward, Jacques Martin, and Norwood's brother and sister-in-law. Today all accounts would be reconciled, and Norwood would attain his revenge.

As Norwood watched Gabrielle laughing, riding astride her stallion in what looked like men's britches, her long hair streaming behind her, his eyes burning with a hateful fire. He mumbled, "And that one … that one I will especially enjoy taming." Norwood signaled to Alf, and he and his men rode towards their unsuspecting prey.

The young women rode at a brisk pace, heading towards the beach. As they approached the patch of forest that separated the estate from the road to the beach, Gabrielle sensed her horse's unease. "There, there, Sebastian, we are almost through to the water," she said, soothing her horse as she continued to ride. Some intuition to be cautious made her turn back to Patrice and cry out, "Let's move about the forest carefully, Patrice." Patrice nodded and slowed the pace of her horse.

The wooded forest offered few paths to the beaches, and only those who knew the forest well were able to navigate them. Midway through, a sound, something like carriage wheels breaking tree limbs, startled them, and Gabrielle quickly pulled her reins, prepared for Sebastian to rear up on his hind legs. Patrice, who was not as adept a rider as her friend, was forced to stop short and tumbled off her horse. Gabrielle called to her as she was several yards away.

"Patrice, are you alright?"

Patrice got up slowly, laughing, and began brushing off her riding habit. "I'm fine. What on earth do you suppose so frightened Sebastian?"

And just then the source of the sounds that the horse and rider heard became apparent. The women were quickly surrounded by two riders on horseback, and one carriage with two large men sitting up front. They looked to be a band of ruffians. Seated next to him was a hooded man, portly, with beefy hands. His face was covered by a scarf and hood. The oaf spoke first.

"Come down quietly from your horses and you won't be hurt."

Trying to keep composed, Gabrielle's heart raced, thinking about the best course of action given these circumstances. "I will certainly do no such thing! You fools are playing a very dangerous game. The Duke of Montrose, my *husband* is right behind us, and he will have all your heads!"

"So, you're going to make it difficult for us, eh?" the oaf responded. He passed over the reins of the carriage to the hooded man, as he leapt to the ground. Pulling out a pistol from the waistband of his trousers, the oaf pointed its barrel squarely at Gabrielle's chest. Gabrielle defiantly held his threatening gaze, grateful she was sitting astride Sebastian, as her knees turned to jelly from fear. With a haughty tone that belied her fear, Gabrielle drew herself up. "You are going to be sorry for this, you brute. My husband will have you hanged if you don't let us go right now."

The oaf smiled as he took a step closer, the weapon leveled directly at Gabrielle's heart. "Get down right now or I will shoot."

Gabrielle remained defiant, lifting her trembling chin a bit higher at the threat, instinctively knowing that they would likely suffer a worse and terrible fate once she surrendered to these men. The large oaf smiled and said, "Let's try this instead."

The oaf took another step closer to Gabrielle, holding her gaze the entire time, and then suddenly lowered his arm and shot Gabrielle's beloved Sebastian in the head. The poor animal immediately fell, taking Gabrielle with him. Patrice and Gabrielle both screamed as Gabrielle hit the ground, her right leg pinned beneath the poor animal.

The oaf then turned his red face to Patrice, and roared, "Now get over here or the next time it will be you I shoot."

Patrice had no choice but to comply, and her own horse now terrified, immediately took off in the direction from where they came. The other two of Norwood's men having arrived on horseback, helped the oaf lift Sebastian off Gabrielle's leg. Once she was freed, they quickly bound Gabrielle's hands behind her back, and blindfolded her as they had Patrice.

Gabrielle was hurt; her leg was throbbing with the pain of having taken the brunt of Sebastian's fall, but she did not think it was broken. Her mind worked on the highest alert. Gabrielle decided to pretend that she could not walk as that might provide her with an opportunity to escape. Unfortunately, it also meant she had to be carried by the man who had just murdered her beloved Sebastian. He lifted Gabrielle as if she weighed no more than a sack of potatoes and dropped her unceremoniously into the back of the wagon where Patrice was likewise forced to lie down. They were covered with burlap sacks which smelled of mildew and old hay.

The carriage began moving, in what direction Gabrielle could only suspect. The scoundrels could be moving anywhere except towards Montrose estate. Gabrielle reached out her bound hands to try and touch her friend, turning over until she felt Patrice's arm.

After a struggle, Gabrielle was able to spit out the gag

from her mouth. "Patrice, are you alright?" she whispered. "Are you gagged?"

Several seconds ticked by before Patrice was able to respond. "Yes, they gagged me. Thank God I was able to spit out the foul rag. I am fine, how is your leg?" Patrice whispered back.

The sounds of the carriage driving over the unpaved roads covered their hushed words. "Fine, but I will not be able to run," Gabrielle replied, "and I don't want them to discover that I can even walk on it. Patrice, I am worried that they will try and ransom us … or something worse. We must escape. Try and see if you hear sounds of water or anything that can describe where we might be."

But under the burlap covers, and the sounds of the wheels driving over rocks and other debris, they could not make out a single thing.

BETRAYAL REVEALED

The carriage bumped and jostled Gabrielle and Patrice for what felt like hours. The women's arms and bodies ached, having been bound during the tumultuous ride. All the while, they tried unsuccessfully to loosen each other's bindings, but could not manage to remove them.

Finally, the carriage came to a halt. The women, who were laying back-to-back, grasped each other's hands, trying to steady their nerves. The oaf and his henchmen yanked the women out of the carriage and hustled them first over the soft ground of the forest floor, and then onto what felt like hardwood planking. *We must be in some sort of house or shed*, Gabrielle thought. They were led across a room and then, judging by the knock against Gabrielle's shoulder, through a smaller doorway into another chamber. The air was stale and reeked of mildew. The women were thrown unceremoniously onto a large bed, its metal springs digging into their backs as they landed. The musty smell of the room and bed was enough to make them gag. Beside her, Gabrielle heard Patrice whimper painfully. Her own leg still throbbed where Sebastian had fallen on it.

"Please," she said with more sternness than she felt, "Surely you can now take our blindfolds off. We cannot be a threat to you any longer." She heard the soft whispers of the men to one another until finally the one who must be their leader answered gruffly, "Go ahead and remove their blindfolds. They may as well see who they will be serving from now on."

The blindfolds were pulled roughly from their eyes, leaving their hands still bound; Gabrielle and Patrice both cried out when they saw their captor.

"Uncle!" Patrice cried out, "How could you! Have you no shame? Have you no honor or respect for your wife and her family?"

Norwood, sweating profusely, leaned in until he was practically touching Patrice's tiny nose with his bulbous one. His tone, though hushed, was low and dangerous. "Do you think I give a damn about your shabby family? First, your grandfather promised me your mother, a beauty, not unlike you, and instead, I was saddled with that ugly duckling of a sister while your grandfather allowed your mother to marry that lowborn simpleton Corchoran! And then I was humiliated in all of London again when this bitch's father," he pointed to Gabrielle, "had dared to remove me from London's waterworks!! I am Alfred Norwood, the most powerful man in London and I must endure a barren spinster as a wife, and now find myself at the whim of the Martin family? I will exact my vengeance on all of you. The Martins, Corchorans, Sinclair and Stalward will despair at losing their duchess and your parents and grandfather will mourn you, Patrice. All my humiliation and grief shall be wrought upon them tenfold."

Just then, Norwood lunged forward, grabbing Patrice's breast. She screeched, writhing against the pain and shock. Gabrielle, sensing Norwood's intention, kicked at Norwood with all her might and he, unprepared for the assault, fell to the ground headfirst, groaning as he did so. The other man in the room stepped into action, and slapping Gabrielle hard with the back of his hand and jarring her into silence. Patrice, horrified, tried to reach over to her friend now restrained by Norwood's brute.

"Gabrielle? Answer me!" Patrice cried, but Gabrielle had mercifully passed out.

The sun broke through the Montrose shutters early that same morning when Gregory awoke to a soft breeze brushing his brow. Instinctively he had reached for Gabrielle, and sighed disappointed that she was not there. Waking up alone was nothing new or worrisome to Gregory, but as the sun began its rise, he grew increasingly anxious at his wife's absence. He dressed quickly, careless of his attire and went in search of her.

After he'd interrogated Alice, his wife's maid, she'd replied cheerfully, "Don't worry Milord, the duchess is likely out riding Sebastian." But Gregory was already out the door in a flurry of anxious energy. Gregory ran to the stables. He knew Gabrielle longed to ride Sebastian since the fire, but he remained adamant that she wait, even on Montrose grounds. Just as Gregory entered the stables, confirming his suspicions upon discovering both Gabrielle's and Patrice's stallions missing, he heard a distant, unmistakable sound that chilled his heart and soul. A gunshot.

James had been upstairs washing his face, when he heard the unmistakeable sound of a gunshot, and grabbed his clothes. Without having fully dressed himself, James made his way quickly to the stables, his heart in his throat. James detected the desperate note of fear in Gregory's bellows as he organized the search party, and was just about to mount his black stallion when he spotted James running towards him.

Gregory's face relaxed only momentarily upon seeing his friend. Mounted now, he gripped the reins tightly calling out, "Make haste James!"

"Where are the women?" James asked. Grim-faced,

Gregory shook his head in answer then turned, leaning his torso low to the horse's back as he began to race across the lawn. James barely noticed that Gregory was wearing only his loose linen shirt half-tucked into his trousers, and no coat at all, as he mounted his own horse and headed off in pursuit. James' mind and heart were wracked with guilt and despair at how he had last parted with Patrice. He tried to push all thoughts of worry and anxiety aside and focus on the only thing that mattered at this moment, finding his beloved Patrice and Gabrielle safe. James mounted his large bay horse and followed Gregory towards the dense trees.

They'd hardly made it to the tree line when out of the woods sprang Patrice's favorite horse, startling the men of the search party. The horse ran for its life, heading back towards the main stables. James and Gregory's eyes met long enough to see the terror reflected in the other's as they continued their chase.

They plunged into the dark woods, silently gesturing for each to break up into two groups and lead the search party's in opposite directions to discover some clue as to the women's whereabouts. It was James, after nearly half an hour, who stumbled upon Sebastian's bloody remains. His heart froze, as he hailed Gregory knowing the horror and fury that would consume the man. And indeed, when Gregory beheld the fallen animal, his lips disappeared into a taut line and his eyes grew clouded with black rage. Without conversation, the men assessed the area where

Sebastian was killed, searching for any hint of the direction that the women and their abductors may have taken.

"Gregory, come quickly!" James called to Gregory who sprinted to his side.

"What is it? What have you found?" Gregory asked. James showed Gregory the recent tread marks left on the white, flat stone.

"By the impressions around the stone," James said, "they are heading southeast, just beyond the beach where the roads lead to the cliffs. They cannot have gone very far." James said this with more conviction than he felt.

Before James finished his sentence, Gregory mounted his horse and sprang off in the direction of the cliffs. James didn't have time to share the other clue he found upon his inspection of the treads — the wheel indentations left by this carriage were a perfect match to the ones he had seen on the perimeter of the Montrose estate following the fire.

A PRICE TO PAY FOR SALVATION

*G*abrielle's eyes creaked open. Her head felt like it was being hammered from the inside out. She thought she glimpsed Patrice in the dark corner, on the floor at the foot of the bed, but could not make out if she was awake or asleep. The room was stifling hot, the shutters drawn closed above the bed. Laying atop the bed was the dark form of a large man that Gabrielle assumed to be Norwood.

Remembering where she was and the events which led to her arriving there, Gabrielle was careful to not make any movement that might alert her captors she was awake. As her eyes adjusted to the dim room, Gabrielle made out more of Patrice's face and saw that her friend's eyes were wide open, fearfully warning Gabrielle of danger. Patrice shook her head slowly from side to side indicating that she ought not make any sound or movement.

Gabrielle's hands remained tied behind her back and she was propped against the wall closest to the bedroom door. After scanning her body for any pain, she was relieved to note that while her head was pounding, the rest of her body was no worse for wear, save her right leg which still throbbed where Sebastian had fallen. Attempting to rally her senses, she searched for some way to help Patrice and herself escape. Panic threatened to surge within her until she reminded herself that Gregory and James would be searching high and low for them and that her husband would eventually discover them. But Gabrielle understood despite that comforting thought, she had no idea how long it would take Gregory to find them, nor what ultimate plans Norwood had for them in the interim. No, she couldn't wait for Gregory. They had to take matters into their own hands.

Gabrielle nodded to Patrice, hoping to signal to her friend that she was ready to make some movement. Patrice squared her shoulders, straightening and nodded confidently. Patrice was ready for whatever Gabrielle wanted to attempt. Gabrielle who blessed the fact that she wore her comfortable britches today, laid on her stomach and as quietly as she could, began scooting herself across the wood floor towards the door. Patrice made ready to follow her, and rolled to her side as Gabrielle had done. Suddenly, a large ripping sound startled them both from just outside the door … the sound of loud snoring. After several tense moments, lying frozen on the floor, Gabrielle determined that the sleeping henchmen weren't awake and wouldn't rouse Norwood yet, either.

Gabrielle scooted to Patrice at the foot of the bed and laid back-to-back with her, working the ropes that bound their hands, trying to break each other free from their binds. After some time, exerting themselves in quiet struggle, Gabrielle's hands were finally freed. The girls listened for Norwood's men. The loud snores from the other room thankfully drowned out the soft sounds of their exertions. Gabrielle turned back to Patrice and finally untied her hands as well. Gabrielle held a finger up to her lips as she signaled to Patrice, and then around the room. Her eyes fell onto a large, empty chamber pot atop a chair next to the bed.

As carefully as she could, Gabrielle crawled towards the chair. When she finally was in the position to be able to reach the chamber pot, Gabrielle turned to Patrice, pointing first to the pot, then back to herself, and finally miming her hitting Norwood who lay snoring loudly on the bed. Patrice nodded. Gabrielle then pointed to Patrice, and then at her own eyes, finally back towards the bed and then directly up above to the shuttered windows, their intended escape route. Patrice nodded.

Patrice then slowly and carefully raised herself up to her knees and peeked over the bed to ensure that Norwood remained asleep. Countless seconds seemed to pass until finally Patrice leaned back down facing Gabrielle and placed her hands together to rest on her cheek as she closed her eyes. Norwood was sound asleep.

Gabrielle did not hesitate, rising quietly and quickly, as did Patrice. Once she stood squarely onto her sprained leg, Gabrielle slowly raised the bowl overhead, looking down upon Norwood's ugly face as he slept soundly, snoring quietly and steadily. Gabrielle held her breath as she timed the men's snoring just outside the room, to when she would crash the bowl down onto Norwood's head, praying that the loud snores would drown out the crash and any cries for help that Norwood might make.

Patrice, had in the meantime, come round the bed, having taken off her filthy jacket and balled it into her hands in wait. Gabrielle understood her friend's intent, and after taking one long drawn breath in Gabrielle crashed the bowl over Norwood's head in time with the snoring of the men coming from the other room. Patrice then quickly stuffed the jacket into his mouth in case he cried out. Luckily, the shock of the attack had rendered her uncle seemingly lifeless.

The women held their breaths waiting to see if there was stirring from the other room. Mercifully, the sounds of snoring resumed. The women knew that they had no time to waste. They climbed up passed Norwood's prostrate form, and reached for the closed shutters, opening them wide. Gabrielle locked her hands together and whispered, "Quick let me push you up."

Patrice hesitated for a moment, clearly worried to leave

her friend behind but knowing that this might be their best chance to seek help, before quickly complying as she was the one most fit for the long run. Gabrielle heaved Patrice as best as she could, and Patrice managed to pull herself up and through the window.

After several tense moments, Patrice whispered, "Gabrielle, come!"

Gabrielle tried to leap up with her good leg to reach the window but to no avail. "Patrice," she whispered, "Go! Go and fetch help!"

Gregory and James both had the look of savages as they continued to crash through the woods searching for signs of Gabrielle and Patrice. They followed the trail of the wagon as much as they could and then used their own deductive reasoning to pursue a path they prayed was in the same direction as the women.

It had grown dark hours earlier, and one of the stablemen called out to his lord asking if they should return for the evening. Gregory and James roared back together *"No!"*

The men pressed forward, searching for some trace of the women. They knew that it would be impossible for bandits to have taken the women too far by carriage, so they looked up at the sky in hopes that smoke or light would highlight their path.

Patrice ran as fast as her feet could carry her. She hated leaving her beloved friend behind at the hands of her uncle and his men, but she had no choice, and she could not fail now. Patrice ran for her very life. Her feet, in her uncomfortable riding shoes, felt bloodied and blistered, she nevertheless hastened on. She knew not what the brutes would do to Gabrielle when they realized what had happened to their master. Darkness had fallen completely about her, and she tried desperately to ward off low-hanging branches and curls of tree roots that would trip her or hinder her progress. She fought the desperation rising and, though her heart pounded, she was exhausted and filthy. Tears pressed at the corners of her eyes. How on earth would she find her way back to Montrose in this blackness?

Suddenly she heard riders; they were close. Staggering to her left, Patrice found a fallen tree stump, clambering behind it as she tried to assess her options. Had the bandits woken up? Was Norwood behind her? She had no way of knowing if the riders she heard were her saviors or her captors. Her breath came in ragged, sharp gasps which she tried to muffle. She saw two dark forms approaching, bent low on their large stallions. No, these were not the weak-kneed men in Norwood's commission, nor the fat large oaf. These were the forms of men of substance and strength.

Patrice sprang up and called out to the riders, *"Here! Here! James, I am here!"*

James heard the cry immediately and pulled hard on his horse's reins. *"Patrice? Patrice!"* he cried.

"James! I am here!"

James followed the sound and upon reaching her, dismounted his horse and ran to Patrice, gripping her firmly as he kissed the top of her head, daring not to let her go.

"Thank God," James whispered. Patrice sobbed in relief and then pulled herself away enough to look up into his face.

"James, we must rescue Gabrielle! She was hurt and could not escape with me. We must go now!"

Just then Gregory found the couple. "Patrice, thank God." Gregory's eyes searched the area anxiously. "Where is Gabrielle?"

Before Patrice could answer James interjected. "She is still being held captive. Patrice, guide us to where they are holding her." James mounted his steed first and then easily pulled Patrice up to his lap. Gregory rode somberly alongside them, and before too long their eyes caught sight of a small structure. Patrice silently pointed, alerting them that this was indeed the place where she had been held, and where Gabrielle would be delivered.

James cautioned Gregory to be patient so that they could determine the best way to approach the situation. Gregory whispered to Patrice, "How many men are there?"

Patrice shed another quiet tear as she whispered back, "Four in total … and Gregory … one of them is my uncle, Norwood. I think he is to blame for the fire at Montrose, too."

James shuddered and held Patrice close, his anger matching the blaze in Gregory's eyes. Norwood had to be completely unhinged to risk abducting two women who had families and connections, one of whom was a Duchess.

The men dismounted on the far side of the shanty from where the bandits had left their horses and were thankfully quiet at their approach. James handed the reins of his horse to Patrice, whispering, "Take my horse and ride for the beaches. Can you find your way back?" Patrice hesitated and nodded finally. She started to beg him to let her stay and help. James responded firmly, "No, Patrice you must try and find the rest of our search party and bring them here to assist us. Now, hurry!" Patrice set off without another word.

Gregory had already started heading towards the structure when he stopped short. The distant sound of a gunshot echoed around them, freezing Gregory and James in their tracks. It was followed immediately by a gut-wrenching bellow from inside the hut.

"You *bitch*! I will see you dead tonight!" screamed a man's voice. Gregory presumed it to be Norwood. Gregory and James took their weapons out and cocked them into position. Two scruffy, thin men ran out of the shanty and in the direction of their horses. They were running for their lives. Gregory and James allowed them to run off so they could focus on the man who remained inside ... with Gabrielle.

Gregory reached the door of the shanty first and signaled to James that he would breach the structure, confident that James would provide him with cover. The shanty was eerily quiet inside. Gregory took a deep breath and then kicked down the door, breaking it off its very hinges just as he heard another gunshot.

THE VANQUISHING ANGEL

abrielle watched Patrice run into the woods and then as quietly as she could, stepped off the bed to stand over the passed-out Norwood, weighing her options. She wasn't sure if she ought to risk trying to sneak past the three men who were just outside that door, or hunker down and try and block the door from the men outside until help came. Gabrielle knew in her heart and mind that Gregory was close. And now with Patrice free to hopefully expedite her recovery, Gabrielle felt certain that soon she would be rescued.

Gabrielle decided to first check Norwood's pockets in search of a weapon. She felt nothing in his front pockets or coat and wondered if there might be something hidden behind Norwood, but Gabrielle decided she could not risk moving him. Providence was on her side as she spied a gun at Norwood's waist. Quickly she retrieved it, tucking it into her trouser's waist band, and slowly moved the one chair in the tiny bedroom to the door that led to the outer room, pushing it as best she could under the doorknob. Gabrielle listened closely and heard with relief the men continue their loud snores. Gabrielle waited, leaning up against the wall next to the door, the gun cocked and pointing straight at Norwood's head.

Time seemed to drag on when suddenly Norwood began to move and groan "Damn the man," Gabrielle thought as she gripped the pistol, trying to keep the tremble from her fingers, and walked closer to the bed.

"Ah, my head! My head*! Alf!"* Norwood groaned loudly opening his eyes, as he held his head between his beefy hands, finally meeting Gabrielle's intense gaze and roared again, even louder, "ALF!"

Gabrielle did not hesitate; she pointed the weapon at Norwood's leg and shot, hoping to hit an artery. Norwood's shriek of pain was ear-splitting as he clutched his left leg, face nearly purple with rage.

"Lord Norwood?" Alf yelled as he continued to try to break down the door.

As the blood poured from Norwood's leg, Alf yelled, "Let me in, you bitches! You'll pay for this!"

Gabrielle knew that the door would not hold much longer so she leaned against the chair, holding it tightly as she looked back over to Norwood who was trying unsuccessfully to rise while holding tight to his bleeding leg. Gabrielle readied herself and at the precise moment when she determined that Alf moved away once more to charge and break down the rickety door. Quickly, and with all her might, she yanked the chair back and stepped aside. Alf came crashing into the room with so much momentum that he fell onto the bed toppling Norwood over as he did so.

Putting the pistol on the ground, Gabrielle raised the chair high overhead and brought it crashing down over Alf's head, and he fell hard on the floor. Gabrielle retrieved the pistol and emerged from the bedroom like the goddess Nemesis herself, ready to inflict her wrath on the two remaining men who looked on her with fear. They needed no further prompting, and ran out of the house, slamming the shanty door behind them to go in search of their horses and escape the mayhem before them. Gabrielle watched with relief as her two smaller captors turned and ran away, closing the door behind them. Staggering on her injured leg, her breath heaving, Gabrielle limped to the shanty's front door, gripping the door frame just as she heard footsteps behind her and smelled the pungent stink of Alf and Norwood. Gabrielle turned, raising the gun and shot, just in time as Alf made a move to lunge for her. The shot had seared into Alf's shoulder, making him pause for just a moment. In shock and fury, he continued advancing towards Gabrielle. She cried out about to fling herself through the door, into the night when just then Gregory and James burst into the shanty sending Gabrielle sprawling.

"GABRIELLE!" Gregory cried as he ran to her, James right behind him.

Gabrielle, dazed but still lucid, sobbed with relief. "I'm all right Gregory."

James raced past them, and, with the butt of his pistol clubbed Alf's forehead, causing him to fall in a heap at their feet. Gregory and Gabrielle briefly locked blazing eyes, both overwhelmed, and then Gregory demanded in a ferocious roar, "Norwood! Where the hell are you?" He left Gabrielle gripping the reins of his horse as he ran into the bedroom, where he found his nemesis down on the floor, bleeding and subdued. Norwood looked at Gregory and finally was able to whisper, "Help me. She shot me."

Gregory lunged towards Norwood in a furious rage, but James held him back urgently whispering, "It's over Gregory. He can do no more harm". Gregory, realizing the truth in his friends words, sneered at the cowering Norwood, then spat at him in disgust, and turned on his heel, returning to his wife's side, unconcerned for the wretched man's fate. Gregory was incredulous; was it possible that his beautiful Gabrielle somehow managed to subdue not one, but *four* men? But even as he wondered how she could have managed it, gazing down at his beloved wife, who's eyes shone brightly with love and unshed tears, Gregory smiled, fully able to comprehend the strength of Gabrielle's spirit. He tipped her chin up to his and kissed her with a passion that now touched the core of his heart and soul. He could never live without this woman.

She was forever a part of him. His equal, his full partner in life.

James chuckled as he watched the couple embrace, finally rousing them to the present with a cough before saying, "Gregory, I think we have been found out." And sure enough, the search party led by Patrice, who finally arrived barreled in, fully prepared to do battle and assist in the rescue of their lords. Instead, they found the duke, duchess, and Lord Rittenhouse perfectly safe with their captors at their feet.

EPIPHANY AND UNDERSTANDING

Two months after their terrible abduction, so many things had changed for both Gabrielle and Patrice. Jacques, Elizabeth and their dear friends Angelica and Tom Corchoran looked upon the beautiful ballroom at the Rittenhouse Estate, and smiled at one another in unfettered joy.

Today had been a resounding success. The bride was magnificent, wearing a champagne gown with an ivory, silk embroidered train, her chestnut hair laying in soft waves, with just the crown swept up into a braided coif surrounded by a wreath of the most delicate orchids, freesia, and spray roses. The groom basked in his bride's beauty, grace, and strength, his eyes blazing with love and pride as he looked into her deep amber eyes which reflected her own joy and passion in their depths.

Gregory whispered into the ear of his lovely wife,

"Lady wife, I am wrestling with myself to not just whisk you off, here and now, and make love to you outside in our carriage."

Gregory spun Gabrielle so he could hold her closer for a moment, as Gabrielle replied with an impish smile, "Well, what are you waiting for, my lord?" Tonight, she wore a ruby red gown that dipped dangerously low in front, showcasing her fuller bosom. Gabrielle's golden hair was coiffed over just one shoulder in an elaborate cascade of curls and braids with no other adornment. Gregory had smiled broadly when earlier this afternoon he watched his duchess regally descend their long staircase to greet him. She was every bit the duchess he'd always hoped she'd be, exactly the way she was.

"Madame," he'd said as he grasped her delicate hand, "as usual, you are a vision."

Gabrielle in response had pulled her husband by his lapels and kissed him deeply. "As are you, my lord. As are you." She kissed him again, this time teasing his lips with her tongue.

"If we are to be attendants at this wedding, we had best leave now, as I cannot trust myself alone with you," Gregory smiled seductively as his gaze swept to her ripe cleavage. Sighing, Gregory reluctantly pulled himself apart from his wife. Gregory's smoldering look made Gabrielle blush and question her choice of gown again.

"Gregory, I feel like I may be a bit overexposed in this

dress. I was fitted perfectly less than three months ago, but now it seems my bosom is bursting forth."

Gregory stopped her with another kiss. "You are perfect, and yes, the dress fits your, glowing beauty ... quite magnificently. If anyone dares let their gaze linger over you too long, they will incur my wrath." Gregory smiled playfully as they walked towards their carriage arm in arm.

Gregory learned from Gabrielle that she was pregnant with his child the night that they rescued her from Norwood's malicious clutches. The thought that he might have lost not just Gabrielle but also their unborn child, would always be heart-wrenching. But love and time would heal much of the trauma that they had both endured.

That fateful night, two short months earlier, after they had finally all returned back to Montrose Estate, and the captives had been led away in shackles by the London authorities, Gregory had carried his exhausted wife up to their bedroom. He gently shooed Alice away after she had prepared Gabrielle's bath. Carefully, Gregory undressed his wife his eyes assessing her for any other cuts, bumps, or bruises. He was clinical and serious and for a while, Gabrielle trembled from the shock. It wasn't until he settled her carefully into the steaming tub that Gabrielle softly smiled. Gabrielle groaned with delight as she sunk deeper into the warm sudsy water. Gregory took a small loofah and gently washed Gabrielle from head to toe. At last, Gregory having washed Gabrielle's hair, filled the basin that was laid to the side of the tub and rinsed her long golden hair until it was sleek and clean. They did not talk, only listened to the breathing of the other, relieved at their nearness and the fact that they were both home safely.

Gregory reached for the large towel as Gabrielle stood, letting the water ripple down her body. He wrapped the warm towel around Gabrielle's shoulders and slowly began to massage her stiff muscles as she groaned, eyes half-closed. Gregory then found her hairbrush and swept Gabrielle off her feet, walking her over to the settee by the blazing fireplace where he sat her down gently onto his lap so he could brush her long hair. Gabrielle, all the while, said not a word instead just drank in all of Gregory's love and attention.

The fire crackled and Gabrielle's body now warm from head to toe began to feel the soft sweep of Gregory's hands in a more primal way. She sighed and turned to face Gregory, mounting him easily as she slid the towel from around her and let it fall to the floor.

"Gabrielle," Gregory whispered, "Are you sure?" After everything she'd been through, he had no intentions of seducing his wife until she'd made a full and ready recovery. His erection quickly betrayed him and Gabrielle, smiling, kissed him. Gregory groaned as he took one of her perfect breasts into his mouth, as Gabrielle rocked her hips against his, a breathy sigh escaping her lips. Gabrielle dragged her fingers through his hair before finally gripping gentle fistfuls and tugging which proved to be Gregory's undoing. He lifted his wife, helping her straddle her legs about his waist as he walked them over to the large canopy bed. He laid her down slowly onto the bed, before taking his own clothes off and climbing over her. She traced the curve of his shoulders as he bent his head and kissed her from her neck down to the curve of her knees and then back up to nestle at her apex. He was gentle with her, slow and deliberate, his tongue reaching deep as Gabrielle shifted against him.

She'd nearly arrived at her climax when Gabrielle, now longing to have Gregory inside her, pulled him up so that she could turn Gregory onto his back. With triumph and a sly grin, Gabrielle mounted him, sliding onto his full length in one fluid movement. Gregory clenched his teeth, shuddering beneath her as she ground against him. He grabbed her soft buttocks and lifted her in time with his own thrusts, softly grunting each time he slid into her fully. Riding him deep, her eyes glazed with pleasure, Gabrielle reached behind her and stroked between his legs in between each of his thrusts, until she finally gave in to desire to satisfy him in the way he had her.

Without warning, she slid off him, bending her head so she could take his throbbing need in her mouth. Gregory cried out, his fingers clenched in the sheets, teasing him until his breaths came in ragged, shuddering gasps. He'd nearly arrived at his orgasm; she could feel him swell between her lips, and she redoubled her efforts, until he finally managed to choke out, "Not yet. Oh God, Gabrielle, not yet."

She released him at last and Gregory yanked her up to thrust hard into her soft welcoming body. He plunged himself into her once … then twice as Gabrielle found her release, crying out his name as she bounced up and down on his aching staff.

Gregory knew his own release would have to come soon and he wanted his beautiful goddess to find another orgasm with him. He lifted Gabrielle off of him, turning her gently onto her stomach.

"Gregory, please," Gabrielle whispered as he trailed feather-light kisses from her shoulder and down her back. His hands spread her buttocks from behind, lifting her hips slightly, so he could loop one hand beneath her and stroke her delicate bundle of nerves as he slid back into her heated core. With one arm bracing above her, Gregory resumed his forceful thrusts, his hips slamming into her buttocks as he felt her inner muscles tighten. Gabrielle turned her face to the side, skin flushed and eyes closed, breathing coming faster and faster as she neared her pinnacle. After several minutes, the couple rocked as one their breath quickening, until they both climaxed together in joyous union.

"Madame wife, I love you very much," Gregory whispered between each kiss he planted on Gabrielle's long neck.

"As I do you, milord," Gabrielle murmured. Gregory and Gabrielle turned into each other holding on tightly. Sitting up, Gabrielle looked into her husband's eyes, the tip of her finger tracing his beautiful lips.

"Gregory," Gabriele whispered into his ear.

"Yes, my love," he answered gently.

"I have a secret."

Smiling, Gregory opened his eyes. "Oh, yes? And what is this secret?"

"You are going to be a father." Gabrielle said the words confidently, but her eyes showed her concern at how this news would be received so soon into their marriage.

Gregory stiffened and sat up incredulous. "Are you certain?"

Gabrielle blinked and answered, "Quite certain."

"We're going to have a baby." Gregory first whispered this in somewhat of a trance as his hand swept back his hair out of his eyes. Gabrielle held her breath as she waited his response.

"We're going to have a baby," he said again. Gabrielle leaned back into her pillow not sure of his reaction.

"We are going to have a *baby!*" Gregory cried out, now standing proudly, clapping, and then lifted Gabrielle off the bed laughing in utter joy.

That week, having rescued Gabrielle and Patrice, Montrose Estate was filled with relieved family and friends. Angelica and Tom Corcoran arrived as quickly as they could and were invited to stay indefinitely at the estate to tend to Patrice. It had seemed evident to the Corchorans upon their arrival that James Rittenhouse was indeed besotted with their daughter, and though she was shyer in her stares, that she, too, was equally smitten with him.

The two girls sat side by side in the Stalward's drawing room and regaled the group yet again about their unprecedented triumph over Norwood and his evil henchmen. Gabrielle grasped Patrice's hands in hers exclaiming, "How on earth did you escape Norwood's evil intent Patrice?" Though the women had not overtly stated the events that led to Gabrielle being struck by Norwood in a fit of rage, they surmised enough of what course the awful brute was capable of after Gabrielle had been struck unconscious.

Patrice sighed, meeting Gabrielle's eyes with a blush. "Well, it is most embarrassing." Gabrielle looked at Patrice imploringly as did the rest of the group including James. Patrice continued, "Well … After Gabrielle had passed out, Norwood turned back to me with a lecherous sneer. I could only imagine his intent though I still pray I was wrong…"

James winced at this, and his color rose to a deep red as he imagined the danger Patrice had narrowly escaped. Patrice paused and then encouraged by Gabrielle continued her story.

"His putrid hot breath was close enough for me to smell, when he leaned in closer to me ..." Gabrielle clutched her friends hand as Patrice continued, "and just as he seemed about to... "kiss" me, my stomach turned over and suddenly, thankfully I managed to be sick all over *dear* Uncle's repulsive and surprised face!"

Everyone gasped at this as Patrice continued on, "This seemed to extinguish his intent, and he turned his attention to cleaning up his face and clothes. Thankfully, once this task was done and he finished ranting at me, Norwood's thirst and hunger seemed to override his other cravings and so he and his men ate their bread and jerky and washed it down with rank ale until they all finally fell fast asleep." Patrice leaned back calmly.

After a moment's stunned paused Gabrielle burst out with a loud giggle that turned into laughter as tears streamed down her face! Slowly everyone else joined her in imagining the stuffy Norwood being assailed in such a manner by his delicate and beautiful niece. Only James remained sober faced, his concern and relief swept over Patrice and filled her with love.

The day after Norwood's failed kidnapping and Gabrielle and Patrice's rescue, Clara Norwood had unexpectedly arrived at the Montrose house, eager to meet with the duke. Gregory found her anxiously awaiting him in the drawing room. "Lady Norwood, what brings you here?" he asked soberly unsure what Norwood's pitiful wife might be up to coming here at this hour.

"Oh Lord Stalward, please forgive me for coming to you like this, but I am so afraid for your family!" Clara cried as she spilled forth all she had heard that evening in the foyer of her home and how Norwood and Alf had planned the demise of Gabrielle and Patrice and that of the Stalward, Martin and Corchoran families. It seemed the next evening she had discovered that her husband had been gone overnight taking Alf with him, and suspecting and fearing something must be amiss she made haste to Montrose Estate to warn the Duke and Duchess.

Gregory tried to soothe her. "Lady Norwood, I thank you for coming. I am certain your niece, and her parents will be grateful to hear of your concern. They are staying here with us." Clara looked up with surprise at this news that her sister's family were afoot.

"Much has transpired in the last two days. You can rest easy that your husband is behind bars at Pentonville prison where he will await his trial for kidnapping, and attempted rape and murder. I am sorry to give you grief with these tidings Lady Norwood."

Clara gasped at this and then crying, said, "Lord Stalward, please forgive me for not having come sooner. I have lived in fear for my own life. I am so sorry. How is Patrice? Was she or the duchess hurt?" Just then the drawing room doors swung open, and Angelica Corchoran entered quickly, hurrying to her sister's side, followed by her husband and Patrice, having been alerted that her sister had come.

Angelica embraced her tiny, and distraught sister. "Oh Clara, thank God you will not have to live with that brute any longer!" Clara clung to her sister and then seeing her niece Patrice, reached out her trembling hands to her niece's grasping long elegant fingers in her tiny cold ones.

"Please my dear Patrice, forgive me for what he did to you and Gabrielle. Please tell me you are unharmed," Clara whimpered. Patrice gently smiled, reassuring her aunt that she was well. Clara was grateful for the embrace of her beloved sister. "I thought you would hate me, Angelica," she sobbed.

Angelica grabbed her sister's shoulders looking into her eyes, and said, "Clara, long have I known the suffering you have had to bear because I chose to marry Thomas and leave you with the earl. Please forgive *me!*" The sisters embraced again, free to express their affection without the fear of retribution.

Later that night, after a satisfying meal accompanied by plenty of wine, family and friends relaxed together in a warm cocoon of camaraderie and peace that only the closest of confidante's and family's experience in their life. Patrice sat between her father and mother, who each had an arm around her shoulders, grateful to have their child safe and sound in their arms. Gregory and Gabrielle sat on the love seat by the fire holding hands, Gabrielle leaning her head on Gregory's shoulder.

"Does your leg hurt much?" Gregory asked kissing her head lightly.

Gabrielle responded with a soft smile. "I am miraculously healed, milord."

James, who had nearly burst from love and longing these last two days, was the only one who seemed less than fully relaxed. He looked at the party around him and thought, *Well, it might as well be now as ever.* He stood, approaching Patrice, and bowing to her father as he begged for a word with his daughter. "Certainly James," Thomas Corchoran replied with a smile.

Everyone was now fully aware of what was likely to transpire, and as the blushing Patrice left the room with James, Gabrielle gently teased the handsome couple as they made their way to the door. "Now don't you two keep us waiting *too* long." Whispering and soft laughter followed the couple as they made their way out of the room.

Patrice and James walked to Gregory's study down the hall from the drawing room where their friends waited for them. James closed the door firmly behind them once they entered the room. Patrice, whose heart fluttered expectantly found herself suddenly shy. Her mind told her that her greatest wishes would soon come true, but her heart was torn by her fears in case James may not have had a change of heart since last they met alone out on the veranda, what seemed like ages ago.

"Patrice, I cannot contain myself any longer," James started, only to have Patrice interrupt him raising her delicate hand.

"Wait, I need to say something first."

James somewhat flustered by the interruption, immediately nodded in acquiescence to Patrice. "James, I know that with recent events you may be feeling a duty or responsibility to change your mind about the institution of marriage. I understand that you are an honorable man and therefore would feel that this is the right thing for you to offer me given the excitement of the last week, but you need not worry about the fragility of my feelings. You don't have to break vows to yourself." Before she could continue further, he moved before her gripping her shoulders and looking deeply into her eyes with an honesty and rawness that she had never before known from him.

"Patrice, I love you. You are right about only one thing and that is that the events of the last week, particularly the thought of you lost to me forever, has made me realize the futility of denying my devotion to you. I fully acknowledge the total emptiness of any life I could imagine apart from you." James took Patrice's hands into his own continuing as he looked into the warm depths of her eyes, "You are unlike any woman I have ever known. There is no change of mind or heart, Patrice, because I have always loved you and I have always wanted you. Please forgive me for so long battling my feelings for you. Patrice, I want you mind, body, and soul by my side and in my heart for the rest of our lives."

Patrice heard all this with a bursting heart, tears of joy streaming down her face. "There, there my love," James whispered, gently wiping the tears away until her eyes changed from brilliant love to an unbridled passion. She cupped his face between her hands and kissed him leaning her whole body into his. James embraced her tightly to his chest. Patrice pushed her lover over to the small divan in the study and laid herself on top of him, kissing him all the while with an abandon that was breathtaking. James was lost to this woman. He wanted and needed her with every inch of his hard body.

When she started to writhe atop him, James knew he had to stop their lovemaking before they were discovered. "Patrice, I would love to finish things between us here and now, but your parents are down the hall, and a servant could discover us at any moment. My wife cannot be so exposed to censure or slander."

Patrice smiled as her sanity slowly returned with his words. "James, you really are such a traditionalist—" A dawning realization made her eyes open widely as she smiled at him. "WIFE? Did you say wife?"

James gallantly lifted Patrice off his body to sit back on the divan and swept down to kneel before her.

"James?" Patrice placed her palms to her warm cheeks as James reached into his coat pocket and extracted a beautiful ring that belonged to Angelica, which James had borrowed from his future mother-in-law for this occasion, unwilling to wait a moment longer to proclaim his love for this woman.

"Dearest Patrice, you are the love of my life. I want to wake up and see your face for the rest of my life. Will you please put me out of my misery and do me the immense honor to marry me?"

Patrice jumped on him sending James and herself sprawling onto the study floor as they both laughed.

"YES!" Patrice leaned into her handsome fiancée and kissed him long and hard.

EPILOGUE

The moonlight shone brightly over the Rittenhouse Estate. The royal orchestra played a beautiful symphony by Haydn, the melody wafting over all in attendance. All gathered in the ballroom of the estate, enjoyed the celebration. Family, friends, members of society, all admired the newlyweds and their closest friends, the Duke and Duchess Stalward, as the two handsome couples twirled across the dance floor.

Gregory held his wife closely, whispering in her ear, "Have I told you how much I love you today, my brave lady wife?"

Gabrielle smiled back, replying seductively, "Why, I do believe it has been a few hours since last you did!"

Gregory whispered, "I love you, Gabrielle." The couple smiled at each other, their feet barely touching the floor as they sailed another turn around the ballroom.

Just then Gabrielle spied the imperious Lady Deville at the edge of the dance floor, strolling with her peacock fan in hand. Catching her eye, Gabrielle nodded, smiling broadly, which heartily satisfied Dame Deville who returned the gesture with her own nod.

Gabrielle sighed contentedly, and leaned her cheek against Gregory's shoulder, wishing for an eternity in this bliss and friendship, for endless waltzes, for her family, and her love.

Thank you for reading *The Duke's Moonlit Seduction*. If you enjoyed the story, please rate and review it on Goodreads, Amazon, or where ever you purchased your copy of the book. I greatly appreciate you taking the time to do so.

FREE OFFER

Click this link or scan the QR code to get access to a free bonus epilogue, exclusively available to readers of *The Duke's Moonlit Seduction.*

ABOUT THE AUTHOR

 Emme enjoys a busy life in New Canaan, CT with her handsome husband and their two mini Australian shepherds, Leonidas and Athena.

Emme grew up in Queens, NY where she shared a bedroom with her grandmother and spent countless hours gazing out her window longingly, at the distant lights that emanated from the iconic Empire State Building, dreaming of one day living an exciting life in NYC as she would escape in between the pages of one of a countless number of romance novels. Mission accomplished, she now loves her life in CT as an author of several genres, romance being her first hearts delight.